Little League Family

LITTLE LEAGUE FAMILY

Leonard Wibberley

Illustrated by Richard Cuffari

DOUBLEDAY & COMPANY, INC., GARDEN CITY, NEW YORK

Library of Congress Cataloging in Publication Data

Wibberley, Leonard Patrick O'Connor, 1915–
  Little League family.

  SUMMARY: When two brothers become members of the Little League, the whole family becomes involved in baseball.
  [1. Baseball—Fiction. 2. Family life—Fiction]
I. Cuffari, Richard, 1925– II. Title.
PZ7.W625Li   [Fic]
ISBN 0-385-12873-8 Trade
     0-385-12874-6 Prebound
Library of Congress Catalog Card Number 77–12887

Text copyright © 1978 by Leonard Wibberley
All Rights Reserved
Printed in the United States of America
First Edition

Little League Family

Chapter One

Mr. Peter Hurley drove through the city traffic to his home in White's Beach a little numbed by the business of the day. He had, lying on the seat beside him, a thick report he had to read, and he was supposed to start writing a report of his own that evening. A sales conference that morning, at which everyone was excessively cheerful, could not disguise the fact that sales were down, and Pestinock, the sales manager, had made it clear that he attributed that fall in sales to lack of drive by the company salesmen. Mr. Hurley was a salesman.

Mr. Hurley turned the car to the right to get off the freeway, and when he had gone a mile or two on the road heading west he began to be aware of the approach of the ocean. The ocean couldn't be seen yet, but it could be felt—a cleanness and coolness of the air which uplifted his spirits and eased his mind, as if his mind had been wearing shoes all day and he had at last been able to take them off.

Somewhere between the freeway and White's Beach there was an invisible wall through which he passed, moving from one country to another—from a country of business and confusion and pressure into one of calm and ease and quiet. It was for this reason that Mr. Hurley lived at White's Beach, twenty miles from downtown Los Angeles where he worked.

When he got home, Mr. Hurley had almost forgotten the declining sales, the thick report he had to read, and the other report he had to start writing. He drank a cup of coffee, discovered that his two youngest sons were watching television, his daughter was at a ballet lesson, and his wife had something on her mind. They had been married twenty years and, although she said nothing immediately, he sensed that something was troubling her.

"Stop playing Indian," he said (his wife had a touch of Cherokee in her ancestry). "What's bothering you?"

"It's a meeting," she replied. "A baseball meeting."

"Baseball," said her husband. "Left to me baseball would still be uninvented. The last time I went to a game someone from Cincinnati backed into the side of our car in the parking lot. Two hundred and fifty dollars."

"He wasn't from Cincinnati. He was from San Diego."

"I hate Cincinnati, and you have no right to deprive me of my dislikes which are a source of comfort to me," said Mr. Hurley. "What about this meeting?"

"I'll let the boys explain," said his wife and called them. The boys, Rory and Cormac, came in in what seemed to be the only permissible dress of youngsters —windbreakers and corduroy pants. Rory was twelve and Cormac eleven.

"Have you washed the dog?" demanded Mr. Hurley when he caught sight of them, for he knew it was best to get them immediately on the defensive.

"Yes," said Rory. And he added, "Last week."

"It is a fact of life, though unknown to science," said Mr. Hurley, "that a new generation of fleas is born on the back of every dog in America every seven days. If you will wash a dog every six days, it will finally become flealess. Why didn't you wash the dog?"

"I forgot," said Rory. "I'll wash him right now."

"It's too cold right now," said Mr. Hurley. In the silence that followed he began to feel a little repentant. They were very good boys, though it was a life's task and probably beyond him to get them to wash the dog and cut their hair.

"Okay," he said. "What about this meeting?"

Rory looked at Cormac, who was known as Coco, and Coco looked at Rory and, having obtained some mutual reinforcement from this, Rory, the oldest, said, "It's about baseball. There's a meeting tonight down in the city Recreation Department office. We've all been asked to get our parents to come. They have to elect directors or something."

"They have to set up the program. Policies and stuff," said Coco.

"So can you go?" asked Rory. "It's at eight o'clock."

Mr. Hurley thought of the report he was supposed to read and the report that he was supposed to start writing. He thought of Mr. Pestinock and the declining sales figures and his part in them. He thought about the chilly moments that would follow when Mr. Pestinock learned on the following day that he had not yet read the report he had been given.

"I've got a report to read and another to write," he said. "This is the worst night of the week for a baseball meeting. In any case, I don't know anything about baseball. I just like watching it."

He was immediately aware of a slight sadness in the room. That's tough, he thought. The world is full of disappointments and kids have to learn to adjust to them. But when dinner was over and he opened the heavy report in the privacy of his study, he found that it contained an abundance of the important sounding words like "infra-structural complexes" and "conditional viability" and "neopassive loss potential." It was a report by a committee of experts on the problems of salesmanship. Mr. Hurley struggled with it for ten minutes, put it down and drifted into the kitchen, where his wife and daughter were mixing something in a bowl.

"Correct me if I'm wrong," he said. "But this is the United States of America?"

Without looking up from the mixing bowl, for they were well used to these strange questions, Mrs. Hurley said, "Yes."

"And in this country people speak English and write English?"

"Correct," said Arabella.

"And the national game is or was baseball?"

"Right."

"Then I go to that baseball meeting," said Mr. Hurley, "because that report I have to read was written by foreigners—maybe even people from outer space. It got sent to the wrong person. I don't speak that language."

"I'm making a chocolate cake," said Mrs. Hurley.

"Arabella will finish it," said Mr. Hurley. "Come to the baseball meeting because tomorrow I'm going to tell Mr. Pestinock that you insisted on going to the meeting and I had to go with you."

"That would be an outright lie," said his wife.

11

"Only if you *don't* insist on going to the baseball meeting," said her husband. And so they went.

There were less than twenty people present at the meeting held in a rather bare room of the Recreation Department which had on the walls photos of White's Beach as it used to be in the 1920s.

The meeting started with the reading of the minutes of the last meeting and then a very short report by the treasurer who, this being the windup meeting of the previous season, immediately submitted his resignation.

"So he should," said Mr. Hurley in an aside to his wife. "Only two hundred and nineteen dollars in the till. I'll bet he spent the rest of it skiing."

It was seemingly time for everybody to submit their resignation, and when they had all been accepted by the board chairman, he himself resigned and turned over the meeting to Mr. Hugh Anderson, the recreation director.

"Well," said Mr. Anderson, "I want on behalf of the city, to thank the retiring board for the very good work they all did last year in providing a baseball program for our youngsters. There were three hundred and fifty youngsters in the program between the Pee Wee, Farm, Little, and Pony Leagues, and that's a lot of youngsters from a city of our size. The ladies' auxiliary particularly did very fine work and have turned over to us two hundred dollars out of their sur-

plus running the snack stand, so we can start the season with a nice little sum of around five hundred dollars. That's better than we've ever done. It's a first-class effort by the ladies' auxiliary and by the board, and I think we ought all to give them a big hand."

They were given a big hand.

"Now the time has come for some nominations for a new board," said Mr. Anderson. "Would anybody like to come up with a name?"

Three members of the old board were very quickly re-elected, but the other two firmly refused to serve again. Finally, a tall taciturn man called Ed, who attended the meeting in well-washed work clothes which still showed the stain of many splashes of cement, was elected and with one more post vacant, Mr. Anderson said, "Would anyone like to nominate Mr. Peter Hurley?"

Several immediately nominated him.

"Mr. Chairman," said Mr. Hurley, "I can't work on the board. I'm so busy I just haven't got the time."

"Nobody has the time," said someone.

"Everybody's busy," said someone else.

"Wasn't that your kid pitching for the Indians last year?" asked another.

"Two kids, I think—a pitcher and an outfielder," said someone else.

"We'd be very sorry not to have you on the board," said Mr. Anderson. "Everybody's busy. It's just a matter of making an effort—for the kids."

Mr. Hurley looked about, opened his mouth, half rose, and sat down again, saying nothing.

"Do I hear a second for the nomination of Mr. Hurley?" asked Mr. Anderson. The nomination was quickly seconded. "All those in favor, say 'Aye,'" said Mr. Anderson. There was a roar of "Ayes."

"Do I hear any 'Noes?'" There were none.

"Then Mr. Peter Hurley is elected, and that fills the last vacancy on the board, and, I think, concludes this meeting," said Mr. Anderson with a bang of his gavel.

"Railroaded," said Mr. Hurley as they drove back home. "I was railroaded."

"No," said his wife sweetly. "You were drafted. Like Eisenhower and Jefferson and all those wonderful men. Who knows what this could lead to."

"Straight into the State Mental Home," said her husband. "Oh well. I'll attend the first meeting and resign. Bad heart, you know."

"You haven't got a bad heart," said his wife.

"If you looked into it right now, you'd be horrified," said her husband.

Chapter Two

Mr. Hurley worked for the Safehold Container Corporation whose motto was "Put all your eggs in a Safehold Basket." It was a good motto except when something went wrong, which usually happened in the Shipping Department and was commonly acknowledged to be the fault of The Computor.

When Mr. Hurley got to work the following day it was to learn that The Computor had been up to its business of defeating the best efforts of mankind again. It had arranged for the shipment of a large quantity of light styrofoam containers, intended for fragile goods like flowers and eggs, to a New England machine shop and foundry which produced, among other things, six-pound sledge hammers. Mr. Hurley spent an abject morning apologizing to the New England foundry and quarreling with Shipping. In the afternoon Mr. Pestinock sent for him.

"Everything has been straightened around in that New England mix-up," said Mr. Hurley. "The proper containers for the machinery have been sent—by air."

"What about that report?" asked Mr. Pestinock ignoring this. "Have you read it?"

"No."

"Why not? You were supposed to get it read last night."

"I had to go to a meeting last night."

"What kind of a meeting—a sales meeting?"

"No. A baseball meeting."

"Baseball!" cried Mr. Pestinock as if he was not quite sure of the meaning of the word. "What do you mean—a baseball meeting?"

"I've been elected to the committee of the White's Beach Baseball League. It provides a program of summer baseball for kids in our town."

"And you put that ahead of company business?" said Mr. Pestinock. "It's vital that you get that report read. This company paid a lot of money for that report. Did you get started on your monthly sales report? You're late with that—as usual."

"No," said Mr. Hurley.

"See that you get it in by tomorrow," said Mr. Pestinock, closing the interview.

Back at his desk Mr. Hurley found there was a teletype awaiting him from the Hawaiian Orchid Growers Association. They received a number of heavy, wire-cored concrete containers in which to ship a hundred thousand dollars' worth of orchids to their West Coast distributors. These were obviously the containers intended for the New England foundry.

"This is the way the world is going to end," Mr. Hurley said to his secretary who had brought him the teletype. "In some massive goof. Somebody is going to dedicate some great monument to the Brotherhood of Man, press the wrong button and blow the United States clean off the map. Did you call Shipping?"

"Yes—they said The Computor . . ."

"Okay," said Mr. Hurley. "The Computor. They might exorcise that thing. It's obviously possessed by a devil. Get me Hawaii on the phone."

While the connection was being made, Mr. Hurley ascertained on the intercom that there were sufficient flower containers in warehousing to fill the Hawaiian order again, and that there was an air cargo flight to Hawaii that evening that could have the flower containers in Honolulu by the following morning. He relayed this information by phone to his Hawaiian customer, who was somewhat mollified by it.

"What are we going to do with these great concrete things we've got here by mistake?" he asked.

"Can you leave them where they are for a while until I figure a way of getting them back here?" asked Mr. Hurley.

"Okay," was the reply. "They're on the back lot and they can stay there for a few days. No charge."

"Thanks," said Mr. Hurley.

Driving home that evening, he reflected that life, instead of getting easier, was getting more complicated. Either everybody was less efficient or work was more difficult to perform.

When he got home, he remembered that the dog had not been washed and inquired for his sons.

"They're out practicing," said his wife.

"Practicing what?"

"Baseball."

Mr. Hurley reflected for a moment. "It seems to me," he said, "that last week they were practicing basketball."

"Yes, dear," said his wife. "Last week it was basketball. Now it's baseball. After that it will be football."

His mail consisted solely of a circular from the city Recreation Department. It congratulated him on his election to the baseball board and informed him that the first meeting, to decide on opening day ceremonies and fund raising, would be held on the coming Friday. He put it aside and his two sons came in flushed, hungry, and in need of a wash.

"How can you practice baseball in the dark?" asked their father.

"Didn't notice it was dark," said Coco.

"Nobody ever taught you that when you can't see, it's dark?" said Mr. Hurley.

"They had the lights on by the tennis courts and we could see well enough from them," said Rory. "We were just throwing. Coco's going to pitch. He's got a real neat curve. And his fast ball is going to be great this year."

"Who said he's going to pitch?"

"It just figures. He's one of the best pitchers we've got. Everybody knows that."

"Including that umpire he managed to hit on the back of the head?" asked his father. "Have you washed the dog?"

"No."

"There are some things in the world that just don't change," said Mr. Hurley. "That's almost a comfort."

After dinner he got a telephone call from Mr. Pestinock's secretary. She said that he was to catch a plane on the following morning to Hawaii to arrange for the return of the heavy containers that had been sent there by mistake. "But that can be taken care of by telephone," he complained. "There's no need for me to go to Honolulu."

"Mr. Pestinock says that he wants you to go personally because warehousing now says there aren't enough to fill the New England order. The containers there are to be flown to New England, and Mr. Pestinock doesn't want any slip-ups. Do you want me to arrange a plane for you?"

"No," said Mr. Hurley. "I'll handle that." He booked his passage and asked his wife to pack a bag for him. "It should only take a day or two," he said, "but I certainly can't go to that baseball meeting now."

"I'll call and tell them," said his wife. "Don't work too hard over there. Try to relax a little."

"Gee Dad," said Coco. "Maybe you can get in a little surfing."

"Sure," said his father. "Somewhere over there they must have a surfboard with a telephone on it."

"Gosh! Imagine getting a free trip to Hawaii," said Rory. "You've got a great job, Dad. I bet they couldn't trust anyone else but you."

"That's not it," said Mr. Hurley. "Everybody else knows how to duck." Later that night, when he had finished writing his sales report and his eyes felt as if he needed new skin all around them, he looked in on his sons before going upstairs to bed. They shared the same room and they were both asleep. The lights were on. So was the television set though the sound was turned down. The dog was snoozing comfortably on Rory's bed and Coco's pillow was on the floor but

21

he was sleeping on his windbreaker which he had crumpled up under his head. Their clothes lay on the carpet in untidy little piles. Mr. Hurley shook his head.

"They're going to have to improve machines, or the whole world will collapse," he muttered. "Boys are hopeless." He reached over to pat them and turned out the lights. The dog, a free loader from way back, wagged his tail but didn't open his eyes.

Chapter Three

While their father was in Hawaii, Rory and Coco signed up for Little League and were issued uniforms left over from the previous season and assigned to their teams. Baseball was not very big in White's Beach. There was a tug of war between baseball and surfing, though generally surfers didn't play ball and ballplayers didn't surf. This was because surfing was dependent upon weather, and who wanted to stand in the outfield on a hot day waiting for someone to hit a ball out to you when the waves were five feet high and the shape perfect in Paddleboard Cove?

"Nobody," said Rory. "So if you want to play ball forget surfing. Best surf's in winter anyway."

"Water's too cold," said Coco. "When they make electric wet suits, I'll be out there with my ever-loving Dewey Weber surfboard."

"You've got to learn to take a little hardship," said Rory, always anxious for his little brother.

"Later," said Coco. "If you push me too hard right now, you'll leave a scar on my mind."

"Right now you don't have a mind to leave a scar on," said Rory.

The two didn't get on the same team. The custom was for the coaches to go over the list of players and select the members for each team in rotation, tossing up for who got first choice. The coaches knew most of the players, though there were always new youngsters signing up. So they knew Rory and Coco were perhaps a little better than average. Coco was a pitcher with a fast ball and not too much control, and Rory a catcher and a pretty good eye at bat. Rory had hit a home run with bases loaded in an All-Star game the previous year on what he admitted (privately) was a fluke. "I swung late on a fast ball, and it was a change-up," he said.

"Uh-uh," said Coco. "You swung early on a change-up, and it was a fast ball."

Rory was assigned to the Indians, who wore black hats, and Coco to the Yankees, who wore blue. Rory's uniform was too small for him, but his coach, Larry Mack, just shrugged. "Good-looking kid like you don't need a well-fitting uniform," he said. "Now if you were real ugly, I might do something about it."

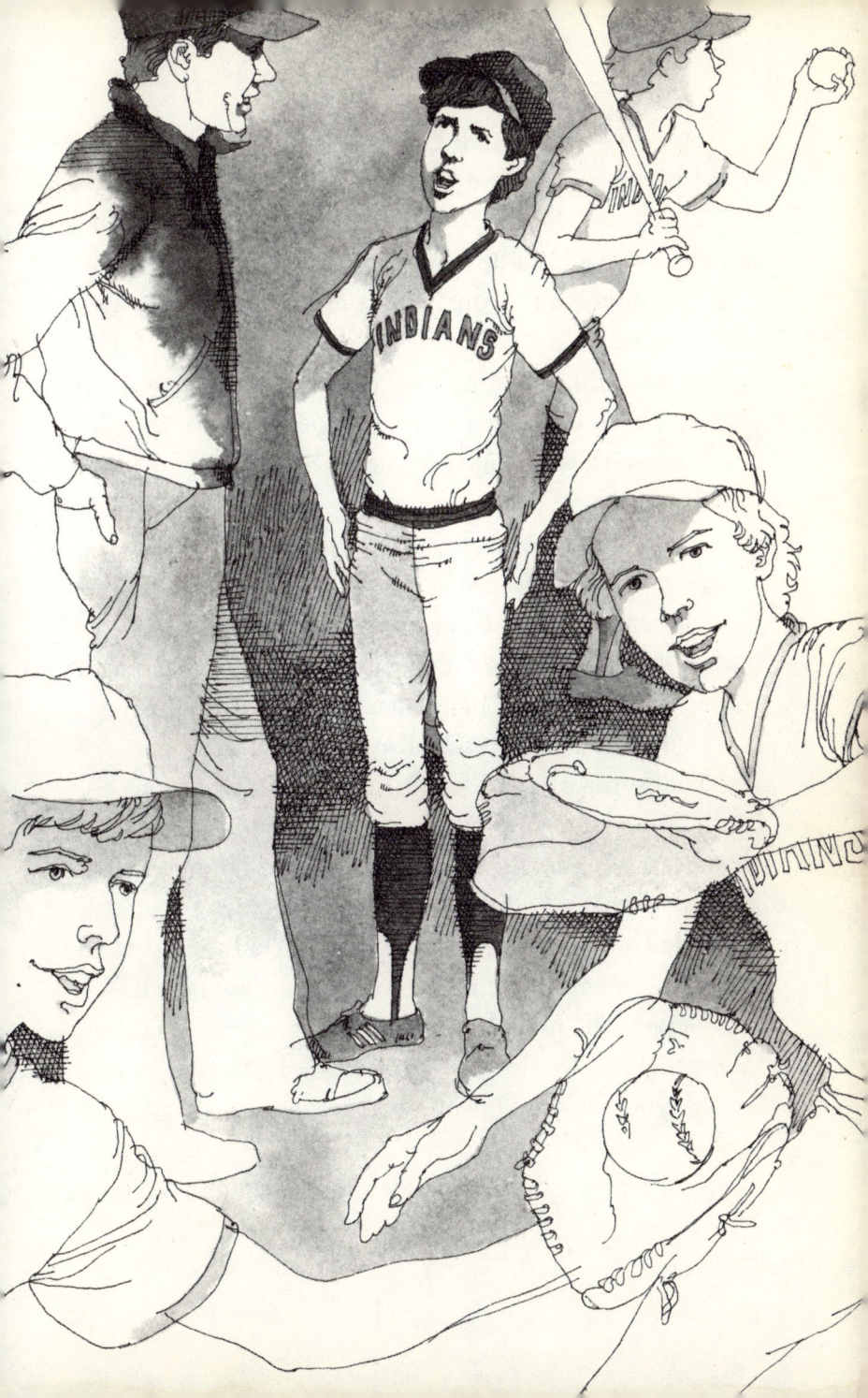

"But how am I going to catch in these pants? I can't hardly squat down in them," said Rory.

"That's one of your troubles," said Larry. "You don't catch the ball with your pants. Just keep that big mitt up there and your eyes open." He looked Rory over critically. "You have got a little winter fat on you," he said. "Do half a dozen turns around the bases. That'll help get you into shape."

"I played basketball all winter," said Rory. "I'm in real good shape."

The coach shook his head. "Get moving," he said.

Coco was luckier with his uniform. It fit him well and it was number three, which was the number his eldest brother, Kevin, now married and living at the other end of the city, had worn years before.

"I got your number, Kay Kay," he told him.

"That's something," said Kevin. "Now if you only had my talent, my perseverance, my dash and brilliance, not to mention esprit de corps and my eagle eye . . . what a ballplayer."

"What a dreamer," said Coco. "You going to be there for opening day with all that talent and stuff?"

"Nope. I'll probably be working. Won't Dad be there?"

"Maybe. He's in Hawaii now, surfing."

"He's *what?*"

"Well, he's got to do something about something

that got lost. But you can't tell me he'd go all the way to Hawaii and not go surfing."

"Well, I'll see if I can make it," said Kevin. "You playing?"

"Yeah. But we're not playing Rory's team. We're playing the Orioles. They have green hats."

"You going to pitch?"

"Maybe in relief. We got a real good curve-ball pitcher. I think he'll start."

"Okay," said Kevin. "We'll see."

The curve-ball pitcher's name was Dale Edwards, and he was from a place called Red Oak, Iowa. He was tall and had very narrow shoulders and had such a curious windup—all elbows and knees—that he was immediately nicknamed Spider. He was a very quiet boy, and his father worked at Interspace Research, which gave him a little extra prestige with his fellows. Besides the curve ball he had a medium fast ball, but his greatest asset was his control. He could hit any point of the target area he chose, and Coco's coach, Tom Pickens (he'd played for the Seattle Seals for three seasons) was impressed.

"Don't try to speed up that fast ball or to throw any garbage," he told Spider. "Just be happy with what you've got, because what you've got is about all we need."

"The fast ball's pretty slow really," said Dale.

"Never mind. If you try to throw harder, you'll lose control. It'll speed up without your trying. In Little League, control is what matters—in fact, in any league. Pitchers who are surprised at where the ball winds up don't last long on the mound."

Coco was often surprised where his ball wound up. It was always a fast ball; remarkably fast. But sometimes it was behind the batter and sometimes so high that the astonished catcher couldn't get it jumping up. In the past, he had had good days and bad. When he had good days he struck out eight or ten batters in a game. But when he had a bad day he sometimes walked a run over and hardly lasted two innings.

"Slow it down," said Rory when Coco showed little control at practice.

"Slow it down," said the coach. But Coco couldn't slow it down. He had a bad habit of not taking his time on the mound, but winding up as soon as the batter was in the box. He wasn't impressive at practice and he didn't improve. In fact, another boy, who had a medium fast ball, proved more accurate and so got the second pitching spot, and Coco was assigned to the outfield, though told that he might be called to pitch in relief.

"If you just weren't in such a hurry," said Rory. "You've got the stuff. You're just too anxious. We'll practice in the driveway at home. I'll catch."

"Who wants to pitch anyway," said Coco, disgusted with himself.

"You do," said Rory. "That's who."

Meanwhile in Hawaii Mr. Hurley ran into problems with the containers. This was his first visit to the islands, and he found that methods of doing business there were very different from those that prevailed on the mainland. The morning of his arrival he introduced himself on the telephone to Mr. Li of the Orchid Growers Association, and said he had come to relieve him of the concrete wire-cored containers.

"Ah yes," said Mr. Li. "If you can come down this afternoon, you can make all the arrangements."

"What about this morning?" said Mr. Hurley. "I'd like to move them out today if possible."

"What's the matter?" asked Mr. Li mildly. "You don't like Hawaii?"

"I love it," said Mr. Hurley. "But the fact is that I've got to get busy with those containers. They've got to be flown to New England."

"Okay, come down this morning," said Mr. Li. "I have an appointment, but you can arrange matters with Boysie. He's the yard foreman. I'll tell him to expect you." It sounded as if Mr. Li added "good luck" before he hung up, but Mr. Hurley wasn't sure.

A stranger to Honolulu and downright scared of the traffic, he took a taxi from his hotel out to the orchid growers' place of business. It lay in a small valley beyond Diamond Head—a vast acreage of lath house structures, lightly overlaid with palm fronds, and below, protected from the slightest movement of the air, what seemed like fields of orchids and other flowers, some growing in baskets and some growing on pieces of wet wood, their roots stretched along the wood like thin, jade green worms. It was half an hour's work to find Boysie, who seemed to have just left every place he was supposed to be. And when Mr. Hurley found him, Boysie, a vast easy-going mound of a man, with a skin the color of cinnamon, couldn't find the containers.

"I think they sent them out to the airport," he said.

"But they told me they were going to keep them here," said Mr. Hurley.

"Well, I think they sent them out to the airport. A truck came and loaded them up."

"Did they give you a receipt for them?"

"Uh-uh. They weren't mine."

"You don't know who took them?"

"No. The driver just said he had orders to take them to the airport. Maybe Mr. Li knows something about them."

"He told me they were out here."

"Why don't you call and ask him?" said Boysie. So Mr. Hurley called, but Mr. Li was away on his appointment. Mr. Hurley tried the airport, but with no luck. Nobody at any of the freight offices he reached knew anything about the containers and nobody seemed to care particularly. Boysie, after forty minutes of telephoning, had long disappeared and when Mr. Hurley inquired for him he learned that he had gone to lunch. It was eleven in the morning.

Frustrated, Mr. Hurley got another taxi and went back to his hotel where he found a message from his home office asking him for early information on when the containers could be expected. It was signed by Mr. Pestinock.

He called Mr. Li's office again and learned that Mr. Li was out to lunch and wouldn't be back until about two-thirty. Two-thirty in Honolulu was 5:30 in Los Angeles, so the only message he could send to Mr. Pestinock was that the containers were temporarily mislaid. He debated between cabling and telephoning, and decided to telephone.

"For goodness sakes, Hurley, find them," said Mr. Pestinock. "New England's messaging every hour about them, and we can't make up the order from the warehouse."

"I'll do my best," said Mr. Hurley.

In the lounge of the hotel he heard his name being paged and checked at the reception desk. "Mr. Li left a message and asked whether you would care to join him for lunch in the Outrigger Room," said the girl. "It's to your left past the elevators."

Mr. Li, it appeared, was a figure of some importance in Honolulu. The head waiter received Mr. Hurley with special deference and conducted him to a table where there was a good view of the hotel's private beach where a Chinese gentleman clad in an expensive white suit was sitting.

"Ah," he said rising. "Mr. Hurley." He paused and said, with a slight smile, "I gather you have been making the usual mistake."

"What mistake?" asked Mr. Hurley.

"Hurrying," said Mr. Li. "You know, it doesn't work anywhere."

"I'm perfectly happy to move slowly," said Mr. Hurley. "But the choice isn't mine. There are other people riding me. The containers are not in your yard, and Boysie doesn't seem to know where they are. They were picked up by a truck this morning."

If Mr. Li heard this, he didn't seem impressed. He passed a huge menu to Mr. Hurley and said, "I recommend the mahi mahi. You can almost taste the ocean in it. And to prepare your digestion, the papaya."

They were through lunch before any further reference was made to the containers. Mr. Hurley had decided he would say nothing about business and see what happened. It was a trick he had learned in the Second World War when he had had some dealings with the British. So, when they had their coffee before them, Mr. Li smiled and said, "You've done well. A good lunch and not a word about business. You'd make a good Hawaiian. Well, then, I have some news for you. The containers were picked up this morning by Flying Bear Airlines and they are at present on their way to New England. The papers are at my office, and I think you will find everything in order. Now how about a game of golf this afternoon?"

"Mr. Li," said Mr. Hurley, "you arranged all this yourself?"

"Yes."

"Why did you let me fuss and fume so much this morning—telephoning all over the place looking for the containers?"

"It's my little hobby," said Mr. Li. "Everybody thinks Hawaiians are inefficient. I like to demonstrate how efficient we are."

"But if you were going to send them back, why didn't you tell me when I called on the phone yesterday from the mainland?"

"You don't like Hawaii?" asked Mr. Li.

"Of course I do," said Mr. Hurley.

"Then let's play golf this afternoon. And in the evening, when it is cooler, you can go surfing. That's really what Hawaii is for—that and orchids."

Chapter Four

Mr. Hurley stayed two more days in Honolulu at the suggestion of Mr. Li. He first called Mr. Pestinock, told him the containers were already on their way to New England by air, and then said that Mr. Li, who was a very important man in the islands, had suggested he stay a day or two when he would introduce him to other men of importance who might have a need for the products of the Safehold Container Corporation.

"You ought to come back here right away," said Mr. Pestinock. "Things are beginning to pile up."

"Whatever you say," said Mr. Hurley, "but I think I ought to impress on you the fact that Mr. Li is very touchy on the subject of Hawaii and he's an important customer."

"What do you mean touchy?" asked Mr. Pestinock.

"Well every time I mention taking a plane back he gets offended and asks, 'What's the matter—you don't like Hawaii?'" Mr. Pestinock reflected that the Hawaiian Orchid Growers account had been worth a steady seventy thousand dollars for the past five years and gave in grudgingly.

So Mr. Hurley stayed on, and played three games of golf, went surfing twice, and went on a tour of the island in Mr. Li's chauffeur-driven Cadillac. He met many other men of influence in Honolulu but had to turn down an invitation to stay over for the weekend and visit the neighboring island of Maui.

"Sometimes I get the impression that you don't like Hawaii," said Mr. Li, though with a hint of a smile, when Mr. Hurley said he had to return.

"I love it," said Mr. Hurley, "but I have a wife and kids back in White's Beach."

"Ah," said Mr. Li, "that is very different. 'The heart away from home withers.' I got that out of an old Charlie Chan movie. I like him better than Kung Fu. You know why?"

"No."

"He was married and had children. Kung Fu is childless. 'The tree without blossoms robs the earth.'"

"Charlie Chan?" asked Mr. Hurley.

"No. Confucius."

When Mr. Hurley left, it was with a spray of orchids for his wife and an invitation to come back soon. "I think you would suit our Hawaiian way of doing business," said Mr. Li. "There are times when I think you like Hawaii."

Back at White's Beach Mr. Hurley tried to explain to Coco that, yes, he had been surfing, and to his wife, that, yes, he had been playing golf. But that all these things were necessary for business.

"Boy what a business," said Coco. "When I'm out of school I'm going to take my ever-loving Dewey Weber over to Hawaii and make me a million."

"Did you wash the dog?" asked his father. The two boys glanced at each other.

"Okay," said Mr. Hurley. "It's a smart man who knows when he's licked. There are some things you just have to do yourself." He glanced with a measure of malevolence at his son's long hair. "Fetch the dog," he said, "and then I want the two of you in the kitchen with a lot of newspaper and a pair of your mother's scissors. We're going to have a dog-washing-hair-cutting session for the next hour or so."

"Oh, Dad," said Rory, appalled. "We'll get our hair cut tomorrow. Promise. Pay for it ourselves."

Mr. Hurley relented. "All right," he said. "But I want it *cut*. Not just shaped and shampooed or whatever they do these days. When a man has gone to the trouble of having both sons and daughters, he likes to be able to tell the difference between the two of them at a glance."

"Boys *are* wearing their hair longer now," said Mrs. Hurley gently. "It's the style."

"Well I don't like it, so cut it off," said her husband.

The following day, which was a Sunday, was opening day for the White's Beach baseball season. The opening ceremonies were held at two in the afternoon with a Salute to the Flag and the introduction of all the teams and their coaches. Everybody was in uniform, and the first game to follow the opening ceremony was Coco's beloved team, the Yankees, and the Orioles. Mr. Hurley found his eldest son, Kevin, at the game, and the two of them sat side by side and studied the players. They were disappointed that Coco wasn't even in the starting lineup, but when after two innings the Orioles hit two "easy out" flies to center field which were dropped, Coco was sent to the outfield.

The Yankee infield had been doing very well, and Spider Edwards had done a first-class job striking out four without any walks. At the top of the fourth it was Yankees three and Orioles nothing. Then Spider showed signs of tiring. He walked the first batter and then the second got on with a stiff grounder that the third baseman couldn't get to.

With a man on first and a man on second a kind of lunacy gripped the Yankee infield. The batter hit a little blooper just over the shortstop's head. The shortstop got it and hurriedly threw wide to second. The second baseman missed the throw, and the lead runner scored. The second baseman retrieved the ball, but, seeing the runner from first already rounding second and the shortstop not covering, he threw to third. It was a good idea, but he threw wild and the ball went to the fence. The second runner scored and the batter advanced to second base.

The score was 3–2, Yankees, with the tying run at second and nobody out.

Spider seemed unshaken. He got two strikes on the next batter who, glancing at his coach, was astonished to discover that he was being told to bunt even though a missed bunt at this stage meant an out. The batter called for time and went over to the coach.

"You mean bunt?" he asked.

"Yes," said the coach. "Just hold the bat level and come back a little. It's easy with a slow pitcher."

If Spider had stuck to his curve ball that would have been the third strike, but instead he threw a fast ball (for him) down the middle. The bunt was perfect. It dropped between the pitcher and the catcher and on the third-base side. By the time Spider got to it he had no play at third and he threw to first. He threw off balance, the ball fell short, and the first baseman scrambling for it missed it completely. The runner at third scored easily. The outfielder came charging in, saw the batter rounding first and threw to second.

It was a good throw but the second baseman was woolgathering and the ball went through. Coco in center field charged for it and threw to the plate, having in the back of his mind the idea that there was a runner at third. The throw hit the dirt in front of the plate and bad-hopped to the backstop. The second runner scored.

"What do you know," said a man behind Mr. Hurley. "A home-run bunt."

"That's Little League," said Mr. Hurley. "You bunt on the third strike and you get a home run."

"That stupid kid in center field should never have thrown home," said the man. "He could have made the out at third."

"That stupid kid in center field is my son," said Mr. Hurley. He turned around to look at the man, a heavy-set individual who grinned at him.

"That stupid kid at second base is mine," he said. "Name of Melotti." He held out his hand.

"Hurley," said Mr. Hurley. "Peter Hurley."

"Nice to meet you. I thought your kid was a pitcher?"

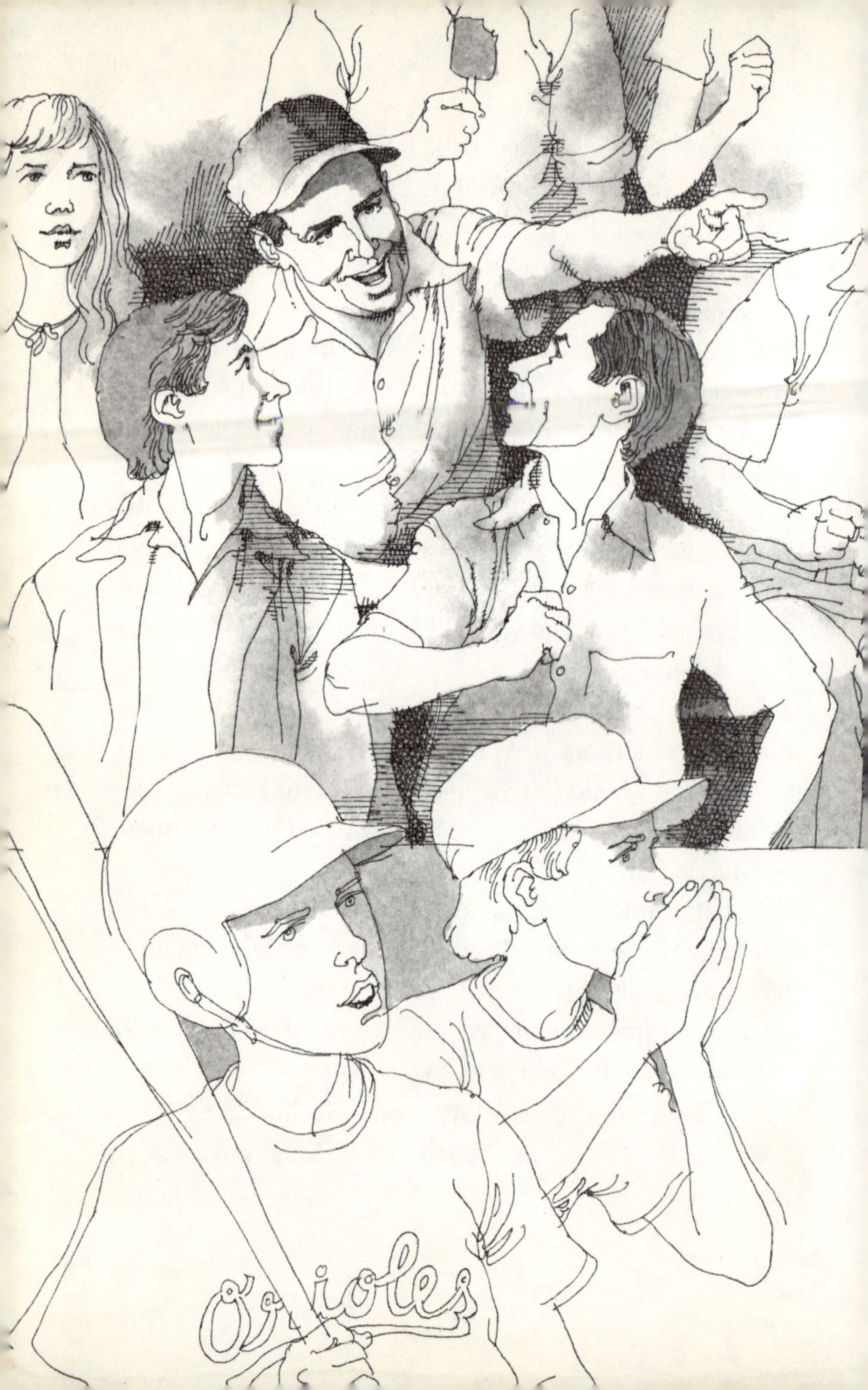
Orioles

"So did I," said Mr. Hurley, "but he's having trouble with his control."

"I'll say," said Mr. Melotti, and then added quickly, "No offense. Great arm."

The score was now 4–3, Orioles, with no outs. Before the end of the inning, Spider loaded the bases and walked another run home, so the Yankees were two behind with the top of the order coming up. There was now a conference at the mound, and the second pitcher was called in. But this wasn't his day. He got the first batter out on a fly ball to third and then walked another run home. The next batter hit a long fly ball to left field and another run scored, so it was 6–3, Orioles. But the pitcher walked the next runner and the coach beckoned for Coco to come in from center field and pitch.

"I've had a real tough week," said Mr. Hurley when he saw his son walking to the mound—looking, suddenly, remarkably small—and heard the Oriole dugout jeering. "I think I ought to just go home and pass out for a couple of days."

"I hope that stupid kid can throw straight," said Melotti behind. "Hey, kid, put it right down the middle."

Coco took his six warm-up pitches of which five were so wild that the catcher just shook his head. The batter stepped into the box, and the first two pitches were both balls.

"Slow down, Coco," yelled Mr. Hurley. "Take it easy."

From the Oriole bullpen came a series of catcalls and whistles while Coco went into his windup. The batter wasn't swinging. He knew all he had to do was stand there and be walked. But the next pitch was straight down the middle and so fast he didn't see it.

"Two more like that," said Mr. Hurley. "Just two more."

The next pitch was a ball, however, and the count three and one. The batter stepped out of the box, glanced at his coach, rubbed a little dirt on the bat and stepped in again. He was hardly set before the next pitch streaked past him and the umpire shouted, "Strike two." The catcher decided to walk the ball back to Coco who took it from him grinning. The batter, to put Coco off his rhythm, took a short walk around the plate and having rubbed some more dirt on his hands, on the bat, and on his pants, stepped back into the batter's box. This time the ball zipped past just above his knees and on the inside corner of the plate. The umpire shouted, "Strike three" and the side was retired.

It was now the Orioles' turn to collapse for a while, and at the top of the sixth and last innings the score was tied at 7-7. But with two outs and nobody on, Coco put a fast ball down the middle that the batter met just right and the ball sailed over the right-field fence for a home run, Coco standing on the mound and watching it go with his hands on his hips. He got the last out with a comebacker and a throw to first, but when the Yankees got up they failed to score and so lost the opener by one run.

Back home Coco explained about his pitching. "Everybody was saying that I had no control," he said. "When I took my warm-up pitches I knew the batter would be watching closely, and I threw wild. So when he stepped into the box, I knew he wouldn't swing. Of course, those first two pitches were balls too. That was on purpose. All I had to do after that was put three fast ones down the middle."

"How did you know you could put three fast ones down the middle?" asked his father.

"Well, just count them," said Coco. "I made twelve pitches altogether. Nine were balls. Three were strikes. Gee any kid can do that."

"Do you suppose he's kidding me?" Mr. Hurley asked Rory afterward.

Rory shrugged. "That kid's thinking most of the time," he said.

Chapter Five

For the next week, things settled down a little for Mr. Hurley. It is true that his two sons, Rory and Coco, were away every afternoon after school practicing baseball, so he got to see very little of them before dinner. His wife was also away an extra night a week on duty at the Little League snack stand. But he had to bring home a great deal of work from the office, and so he was glad of the quiet. Then he got a call from Al Flint, who he vaguely remembered was a fellow member of the baseball committee left over from the previous year.

"Did you get a copy of the minutes of the meeting you missed?" asked Al.

"Uh-uh," said Mr. Hurley. "Figured I'd catch up at the next meeting. When's the next meeting?"

"Not for two weeks. Thought I ought to call you and remind you to get busy on the Pancake Breakfast."

"Pancake Breakfast?" said Mr. Hurley. "What have I got to do with a pancake breakfast?"

"Well, of course, you weren't there at the last meeting," said Al, "but the committee voted unanimously to appoint you chairman of the Pancake Breakfast. That's our big money-maker. Figure on raising fifteen hundred, maybe two thousand dollars if we go at it right."

"One minute," said Mr. Hurley. "You can't do that to me. I wasn't even there. You cannot appoint a man to a committee in his absence."

"That's about the only way we *can* appoint a man to committee," said Al. "If he's there, he usually objects."

"Well, I object. I refuse to accept the appointment," said Mr. Hurley.

There was a tense moment or two of silence. Then Al said, "White's Beach is kind of a small town, Mr. Hurley," he said. "Feller has to watch his public image."

"The heck with my public image," snarled Mr. Hurley. "I'm not going to be chairman of that Pancake Breakfast, I'm too busy."

"That's what I mean about public image," said Al.

"Now you take last year. Last year I was chairman of the Pancake Breakfast. Of course, I'm only a small-time contractor. Didn't do anything else last year but put up two condominiums and the restaurant down at Fourth and Pier and try to hassle with a lot of estimating on other jobs I didn't get. Then take Bob Jones. He handled it the year before. He's the manager down there at the Home Bank, and he said he had the busiest year for loans and whatnot since the bank opened. And you know with so many customers in touchy businesses like aircraft and space and so on, that loan stuff would give an alligator ulcers. Then Marge Wheeler—running that real estate business of hers with five kids and her husband dead and . . ."

"Okay," said Mr. Hurley. "I get it. If I don't run the Pancake Breakfast, I'm a fink."

"Oh, I wouldn't say that," said Al. "I mean, busy as you are going to Hawaii and so on. Your kid says the surfing was great . . ."

"Grrrr," said Mr. Hurley. "Wait until I get my hands on that Coco."

"Need any help, give me a call," said Al. "As I say, I handled it last year and I may know a few wrinkles that may help you out—like in the Recreation Hall you can only use one electric grill at a time because if you use two, it blows all the lights. And you can't get chairs from the Dolphins Club anymore—

they got rid of them when they built that new auditorium with permanent seating. Permaprint might quote you on the tickets as a favor, but they're pretty busy and you need to get the order in early . . ."

"Just a minute," said Mr. Hurley. "Grills, chairs, tickets . . . just how much does this involve?"

"Oh, it isn't that much really," said Al. "You just got to figure on feeding breakfast to maybe four thousand people and a bunch of kids in about five hours—say starting at seven and going on to noon. After that it drops off. There's the food and the dishes and the washing up and cutlery and garbage containers and chairs and tables and so on. If you run into any problem, just give me a call." And he hung up.

For a few minutes Mr. Hurley just stared at the wall, unable to believe that such a thing could happen to him. All he had ever done was innocently attend a meeting on baseball, and here he was about to organize a breakfast for four or maybe five thousand people.

He felt a distinct tendency to panic. He had never cooked breakfast for more than his own family and that only on the few occasions when his wife was away or ill. He started to think about quantities. How much pancake batter was needed for four thousand breakfasts? Supposing he got enough for four thousand breakfasts and only three thousand came—what would he do with the rest? What else went with pancake breakfasts? Sausages of some kind usually. How much sausage? And syrup. How did you estimate syrup? Some people poured masses of syrup over their pancakes, and some people used only a little dollop. Some people didn't like syrup and used butter.

His wife was visiting a friend, so he wandered into the kitchen and opened one of the cupboards. Among packages of cookies, drinking straws, breakfast cereals, and other dry foods with which he had only a nodding acquaintance he found a box of pancake mix. The directions were very simple. Three cups of mix and two and one-quarter cups of water would give from twenty-one to twenty-four pancakes with any luck. Reckon four pancakes to a serving, and three cups of mix would serve six people. Six into four thousand was about six hundred and sixty-odd and that meant about two thousand five hundred cups of pancake mix and enough water to float a light cruiser in battle trim . . .

He reached for the telephone and called Al Flint again. "Al," he said, "Pete Hurley here. If you handled the Pancake Breakfast last year, can you give me a list of the groceries you ordered—how much pancake mix, how much syrup and so?"

"Call Dottie Green. She handled the finances. I turned the whole thing over to her for payment." He gave the number.

Mr. Hurley called Mrs. Green. Mrs. Green said she had the list somewhere, and she would call him back. She called back to say that she just remembered that all the lists had been turned over to Chuck Waller, who had drawn up the annual report. He was an accountant and would have them in his files. She gave him the number.

Chuck Waller said that in making up the annual report he had not been interested in individual quantities but only in general headings—so much for chair rental, so much for groceries, and so on. He didn't remember getting any detailed lists anyway but why not call Al Flint, who had been in charge of the Pancake Breakfast?

Mr. Hurley hung up the phone with a groan. "The good old circle again," he said. Out of pure malice he called Al Flint again, to needle him about the list, but Al said, "You know something? That happens every year. Happened to me. Happened to Bob. People just don't keep records these days. I guess you'll just have to start at the beginning and do your own figuring."

"Tell me one thing," said Mr. Hurley. "Just how many people did you have at the Pancake Breakfast last year?"

"Nobody ever made a count," said Al. "But we took in around about twenty-three hundred dollars."

"Maybe I can figure it from that," said Mr. Hurley. "What did you charge?"

"Dollar apiece for adults, kids under sixteen, fifty cents, and kids under five, nothing."

"Well, do you think there were more dollar breakfasts than fifty-cent breakfasts, or were they about the same or what?"

"Can't say," said Al. "I was busy over a hot griddle. Man but that's hard work. You'll see."

His daughter, Arabella, who had been sewing something in her room came wandering in. She loved, sewing and made most of her own clothes. "What's the matter, Daddy?" she said.

"Nothing much," said Mr. Hurley. "Just a routine disaster. I have to organize a Pancake Breakfast for four thousand people."

"Four thousand?" said Arabella. "Gosh." She went into the kitchen and returned with a packet of pancake mix, which she puzzled over for a moment or two. "You'll need three hundred of these two-pound packages," she said. "That's six hundred pounds of mix. Of course, if you gave everybody three pancakes instead of four, you could reduce that by a quarter, making it four hundred and fifty pounds of flour. That's a good saving."

"How do you know all this?" asked her father.

"Simple," said Arabella. "Right here on the package it says 'sufficient for fifty pancakes.'"

"How am I going to get four hundred pounds of

pancake flour mixed up," asked Mr. Hurley. He thought of some of the friends who might help him and shook his head. "Boy, that stuff is going to be lumpy."

"Why don't you ask Mr. Heinz, the baker, to mix it for you?" asked Arabella. "We went over to his bakery during Home Economics one day and he's got some real rugged mixers."

Her father looked at her in admiration. "Let me tell you something, Arabella," he said. "Anybody who wants to marry you is going to have to pay me around about a million dollars. What were you sewing by the way?"

"Rory's pants. There was enough material to let them out. I think they'll fit him now."

"If women's libbers gain one inch more," said Mr. Hurley fervently, "we men are lost."

Later Rory and Coco arrived back from practice. Rory looked glum. "I think they're going to put me in the outfield," he said. "Coach had me out there all afternoon."

"Who was catching?" asked his father.

"Al Harter. He's a new kid. From Florida, I think."

"That's not fair," said Coco. "You caught all last year. Even on All Stars. Everybody knows you're good. I know that kid. His dad's always in the stands and keeps talking up his son to the coach. He's a big

51

loudmouth. Dad, you ought to speak up for Rory. You're on the board or something."

"Let Rory fight his own battles," said Mr. Hurley.

"Not if he has to fight this kid's dad as well."

"If Rory's a better catcher, he'll get the job," said Mr. Hurley. "Besides, parents should stay out of Little League and leave it to the coaches."

"But Dad, some parents don't," said Coco.

"Okay," said his father. "Some don't, but it doesn't make it any better if everybody follows their example, does it? Who's Rory's coach, anyway?"

"Larry Mack."

"Larry Mack? Never heard of him."

"Dad," said Coco, "Larry Mack's the guy that built that high fence on the corner of Twenty-first and Pier. You complained that you couldn't see around it for driving, and he had to take it down."

"Oh-oh! Well, it *was* too high, and if he did it again, I'd have to complain again."

Coco looked at his brother and shrugged. "It isn't that bad in the outfield," he said. "I'm getting used to it myself. Nice and warm and you get a little exercise running in and out."

"Didn't they let you pitch today at practice?" asked his father.

"A little," said Coco. He shook his head. "Boy, was I wild," he said thoughtfully. "It was either in the dirt or so high it had snow on it. I must be doing something real wrong, but I can't figure out what it is."

"You're going to throw to me starting tomorrow," said Rory. "I'll soon find out what it is."

"I like it in the outfield," said Coco. "No worries, and you still get your ups."

"Your place is out there on the mound—worrying," said Rory. "We'll start practice tomorrow."

Chapter Six

All in all, things were going remarkably well at the office for Mr. Hurley. He went to Portland, Oregon, and rounded up a handsome order for containers for round cheeses from the Oregonian Cheddar Corporation and, following up a lead he got from Mr. Li in Honolulu, he made a trip to the big island of Hawaii to talk to the Coffee Producers Association about putting up their coffee in styrofoam containers instead of cans.

There were three problems to be overcome here—the first a rooted prejudice to putting coffee up in anything but a can; the second the fact that cans of coffee could be easily loaded and unloaded by magnetic cranes, which could not be done using styrofoam containers; and the third the belief that styrofoam had an aroma that would affect the bouquet of coffee.

To this last objection, Mr. Hurley had a sovereign reply. "Millions of cups of coffee a day are served in styrofoam cups," he said. "If styrofoam doesn't affect the taste of the hot coffee, surely it won't interfere with the aroma of the coffee before it is prepared."

Eventually he had several different shapes of containers made up out of styrofoam, each holding a pound of coffee, and shipped these, full of coffee to the sales manager of the producers association in Hilo. He pointed out that the containers were lighter than cans and would save in freight charges and could be handled by magnetic cranes if placed in the metallic boxes that airplanes and shipping companies now used for cargo handling. He felt he had made a breakthrough when he got one order for one thousand oblong-shaped containers of styrofoam, each to hold two pounds of coffee. It was an order so small that his company would lose money on it, but as he pointed out to Mr. Pestinock, "When they come through with an order for a million a month, it will be solid gold for us."

"The trouble with that," said Mr. Pestinock, "is that we're not the only people who make styrofoam containers. Remember Rockefeller and China."

"What about Rockefeller and China?" asked Mr. Hurley.

"I thought everybody knew that story," said Pestinock. "Dutch Shell or somebody heard that millions of people in China were lighting their houses with miserable little wicks of rush floating in a bowl of oil. So they decided to supply them with kerosene lanterns free. They figured that would provide a market in China for kerosene that would make every stockholder a millionaire. They made the lanterns and sent them to China. But Rockefeller came in right behind them and sold the Chinese the kerosene. Catchall Containers may corner your coffee market yet."

"Over my dead body," said Mr. Hurley.

While Mr. Hurley battled with his business problems, and at home attempted to organize a mammoth pancake breakfast, his sons struggled with their schoolwork and their baseball practice.

There was a long driveway beside the Hurley home leading to a garage in the rear. The driveway sloped up to the end nearest the street and so provided the kind of elevation given a pitcher on his mound. Here Coco practiced his pitching while Rory caught for him. The trouble was that Coco was so wild at the beginning that Rory often couldn't catch the ball which crashed against the garage door. The door was of half-inch planks laid horizontally across a frame.

At first it showed only a few scuffs and dents from the ball. But after a week of this kind of hammering, one of the planks split and Mr. Hurley came home one evening to find a hole battered in his garage door. The neighbors also started to complain about the noise.

"Can't you pitch somewhere else?" he demanded. "What's wrong with the park?"

"Dad, if we go to the park, other kids come along and pretty soon we're not pitching, we're playing some kind of ball game. You just can't practice at the park."

"Well, rig some kind of a backstop other than the garage door," said Mr. Hurley. "Hang up that old sail off the dory." But the old sail off the dory only lasted two days when it was ripped to tatters. Some old curtains fared no better.

"What about the mattress on your bed?" said Coco.

"What about the mattress on *your* bed?" said Rory.

They settled the problem by using the mattress on a foldaway spare bed. But between wild throws and passed balls, the flocking was soon spilling out of this. They appealed to their elder brother, Kevin, who found three bales of straw for them, but, though better than anything tried so far, the bales started to fall to pieces under the constant battering. The final solution was the three bales of straw wrapped in an old carpet.

"Gosh," said Coco after all this trouble. "All you got to do is catch the ball."

"Give me a chance," said Rory. "Keep it in the same town, will you?"

It developed that Coco during the off season had picked up two bad faults. He was releasing the ball too early and he was trying to throw too hard. When he overcorrected on the release he threw the ball into the dirt. After a few days of this without much improvement Rory called Kevin, who had done some pitching in college.

"You see what you can do with him," he said. "He was a good little pitcher, but I just can't get him to settle down this year."

"How are you doing yourself?" asked Kevin.

"Oh, I'm in the outfield now."

"Not catching?"

"No. They got a real good boy for catcher. He's better than me. No kidding."

Kevin said nothing but addressed himself to the problem of Coco's pitching.

"Coco," he said, "you're only eleven so you've got a good ten years to go before you're in the majors. So take your time. Just concentrate on throwing the ball and hitting my glove. Nothing more. Never mind how fast or how slow or whether it's a curve or a slider or whatever. Just hit the glove. No windup. Just throw."

To Coco's disgust, Kevin practiced him at this for a

week. But he had to admit that at the end of it, his accuracy had improved enormously.

"Now, still no windup, throw a curve and hit my glove," said Kevin.

"But I got to wind up," said Coco.

"No you don't," said Kevin. "The windup's the spring. It's what gives you the speed. It's nothing to do with aim. Right now what you need is accuracy. You're getting better. Have you noticed where your hand is when you release the ball?"

"Uh-uh," said Coco.

"Great," said Kevin. "Right now you're replaceable by a monkey. How about watching and thinking?"

So Coco watched and thought and discovered that accuracy meant keeping his eye always on the target and following through so that his pitching hand wound up pointing to the target—Kevin's glove in this instance. He had known this instinctively before, but now he knew it consciously, and when his throwing began to get wild, he had at least two points to check in locating the trouble.

After several days of throwing from a standing position without a windup, Kevin let Coco try winding up. For a day or so he was as wild as ever. Then his accuracy returned and he could deliver a good fast ball with plenty of "weight" in it and right on target.

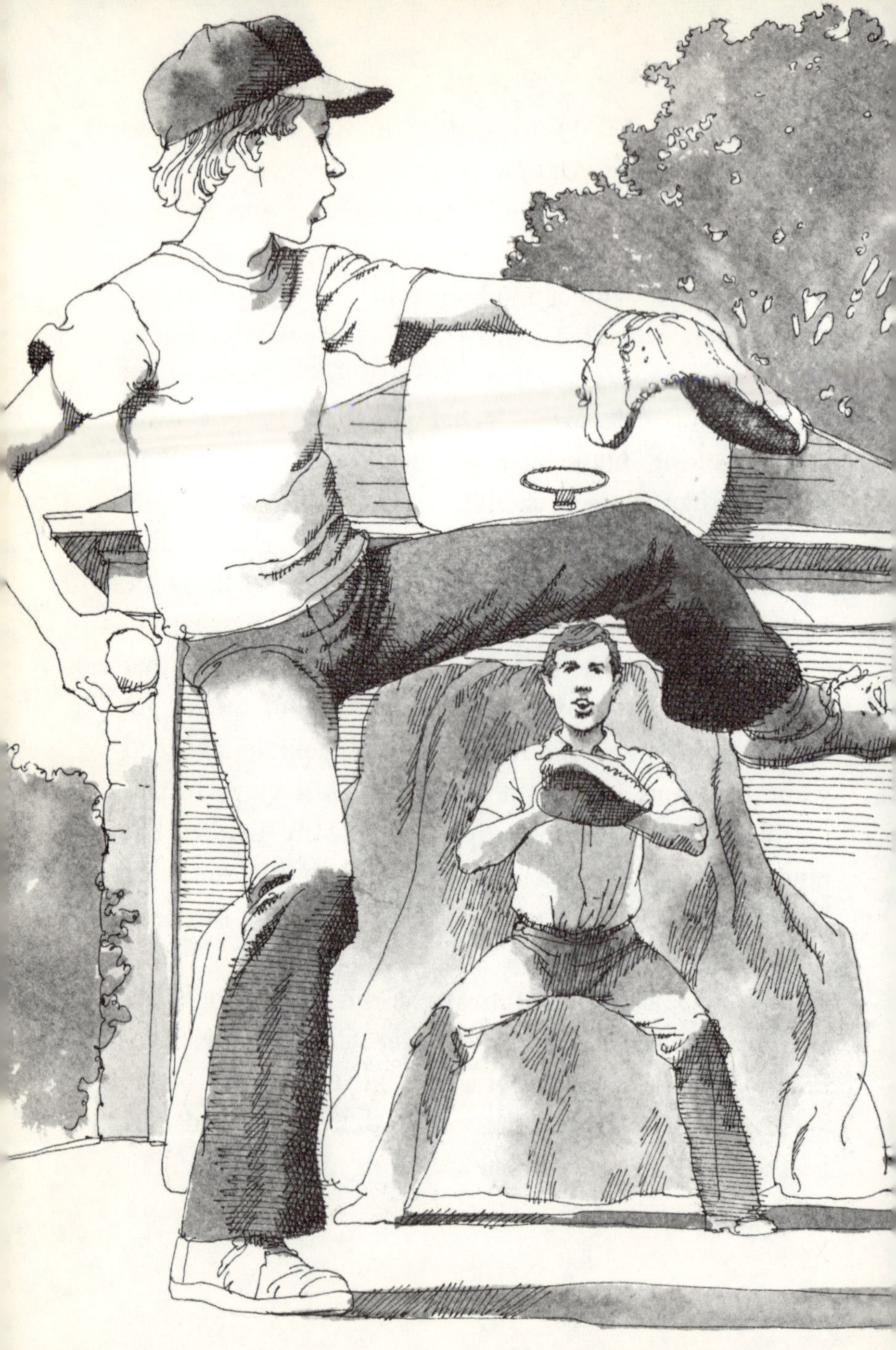

"Remember this," said Kevin. "In Little League the most important thing for a pitcher to do is throw strikes. Never mind the garbage—the curves and slider and so on. If they come naturally, fine. But just try for strikes with a medium ball and a change-up. That's all you need. It isn't Henry Aaron you're pitching to, you know. You'll get hit, of course. But you'll get a lot of strike-outs as well. And when they hit you, there are seven other guys out there fielding. You don't have to strike out everybody."

"When you were pitching at college, did you plan on the ball getting hit?" asked Coco.

"Sure," said Kevin. "I had a great outfield. Next time you're watching a game on TV, just count how many outs there are on long fly balls."

"Lots of home runs too," said Rory.

"Home runs are accidents," said Kevin. "When you're pitching, forget about them. If they were important in a pitcher's career, they'd keep statistics on how many home runs got hit off of particular pitchers. They don't. If you think about it, most ball games—Little League or Major League—are won or lost on errors. Fumbled balls. Dropped balls. Double plays missed. Balls thrown away, and pitching errors."

"Pitching errors?" asked Coco.

"When a pitcher walks a guy that's an error on the pitcher, though they don't score it that way," said Kevin.

61

The first meeting between the Yankees and the Indians—between Coco's team and Rory's team—found both brothers playing center field despite all their practice. Coco, who was by no means bashful, told his coach that he had been doing extra pitching practice and was getting pretty good.

And his coach grunted and told him to stick around and help police the grounds after the game.

Spider Edwards had pitched his full game for the week, so Chuck Podranski opened for the Yankees, and at the top of the fourth it was Yankees 5, Indians 1. Chuck was having a good day, though most of the Yankee runs had come on fielding errors. Then the Indian infield, which had let too many balls go through, settled down to business.

The third baseman, seemingly to his astonishment, caught a line drive high and to the left of the bag and had enough of his wits left to throw to first to catch the runner who didn't get back in time. The next batter was walked and took second on a passed ball, but the next was out with a comebacker to the pitcher and the side retired.

It was the top of the order for the Indians as they came up to bat—Ken Ishiwara, first baseman, then Joe Springer, a stocky little guy with big shoulders and stubby arms, and then Al Harter, the catcher from Florida, followed by Rory in cleanup.

Ken Ishiwara elected to bat left-handed, and Podranski walked him. Springer hit a change-up over the third baseman's head putting a man on first and second. Harter got the signal to bunt, missed twice and, with the count three and two, was walked loading the bases.

Rory came to the plate with his stomach feeling as if someone had been punching him in it, and his mouth strangely dry. He had only one thought, which he tried to keep under control, and that was "Home Run."

"No outs," said Larry Mack, his coach. "Don't try to be a hero. Just poke it through somewhere and get on base." There was a short conference at the mound and Coco, who was wondering whether Rory was likely to try for his home run in his direction, saw the second-base umpire signaling him.

"Oh no," he said to himself. "Bases loaded, nobody out, and Rory at the plate."

"You're on," said the coach, giving him the ball.

"Coach," said Coco. "Good old Spider can still pitch an inning or two under the rules."

"You're on," said the coach grimly. "I thought you said you'd been practicing?"

"Coach," said Coco, "the batter's my brother. He's been catching me and watching me. The bases are loaded and he can hit anything I can throw."

63

"You wanted to be a pitcher," said the coach. "You figure it out."

Coco took his six warm-up pitches and Rory, standing in the batting circle took a practice swing at each of them, grinning all the while.

Chapter Seven

Before he stepped into the batter's box, Rory glanced at the batting coach. He saw him wipe his hands on the front of his jacket, touch the bill of his cap and then clap his hands together four times. The fourth clap meant that he was to swing at anything he liked, the rest being a mere show to mystify anyone who might be watching. Rory choked up on the bat and took his stand. Coco shook off several signals from the catcher and then walked toward home plate to meet him after calling for time.

"I'm going to walk him," he said.

"That'll walk a run home," said the catcher.

"I know," said Coco. "And it's his chance for a home run, and he'll kill me. But he can hit almost anything I put over the plate."

"Gosh—you going to walk home a run?"

"Yes," said Coco. "That'll make it five to two, our favor. But if Rory hits a homer it'll be five all."

"Okay," said the catcher. "But you'll still have bases loaded."

"I was doing so good in center field," said Coco and walked back to the mound. But now the catcher instead of squatting behind the batter, stepped a little to the side and held down an arm. A groan went through the crowd interspersed with catcalls. Coco threw the four balls, Rory glared at him, and walked sullenly to first base, and the run came home making the score Yankees 5, Indians 2.

Mr. Hurley, who had been delayed at the office, had just joined the spectators and somebody said to him, "Your kid just gave an intentional walk to his brother with bases loaded. Walked a run home."

"Any outs?" asked Mr. Hurley.

"No."

Mr. Hurley glanced at Coco out on the mound. He seemed very small. The batter seemed very big. He felt a tightening of the muscles of his stomach and an uneasy feeling crawling up the side of his neck.

"I think I'll go home," he said. "I had a bad day at the office."

But he sat down anyway and watched Coco, after shaking off two signals, go into his windup. It was a beautiful pitch, straight down the middle with a slight inside curve. But it wasn't good enough. The batter stepped up to meet it, swung, and with a satisfying "click" the ball soared up and away toward the right-field fence. The right fielder came forward to meet it, hesitated, moved back and then darted forward again. For a moment he seemed to have lost sight of the ball, but he caught it, tripped, fell, and came up with the ball in his hand. The runner on third held.

One away.

On the mound Coco heaved a sigh of relief and straightened out the dirt in front of the rubber. He hoped nobody could see that his knees were trembling slightly. He glanced over at the third baseman, who stared solemnly back at him, sighed, stepped on the rubber and went into his windup. He deliberately threw a ball—high and outside, but not so wide the catcher couldn't get it with ease. Then he threw another, only that one wasn't deliberate.

"That stupid kid can't pitch," said Mr. Melotti, who was once again sitting behind Mr. Hurley.

"That stupid kid is my kid," said Mr. Hurley.

The next two pitches were strikes, one low on the inside corner and one (a little dubious from the stands) high and on the outside corner.

"One more like that Coco," shouted Mr. Hurley. "Just one more."

With the count two and two and the bases loaded, the batter looked to the coach. Whatever the signal was, Coco was sure he was going to swing. He went into his windup and threw fast and right down the middle but low. The batter swung and missed and it was strike three and one more to go. The catcher ran the ball back to Coco.

"You're doing great," he said. "How do you feel?"

"I feel like I've been out here since last Christmas," said Coco. "Who's this guy coming up?"

"Christoferson. Keep it low. He'll swing at anything high, and he's got lots of power."

Coco decided that, this being a last chance, the batter was likely to swing at anything he liked, ball or strike. The first pitch was in the dirt but the catcher got it. Ball one. The second pitch was called low and that was ball two. The third pitch was a strike, a change-up which completely fooled the batter who swung well ahead of it. The next pitch was letter high and right down the middle—a direct challenge to the batter. He swung, but his timing was off and he fouled the ball over the backstop. The count stayed two and two.

Coco could choose now whether to throw a strike or try to fool the batter into swinging on a ball. He decided to throw a strike, a plain ordinary strike right down the middle; and he was well into his stretch before he remembered Kevin's repeated warnings against trying to throw hard.

So he took something off it, and the ball completely fooled the batter. It seemed to float from Coco's hand toward the plate and dance a little in the air. The batter swung too early and struck out, and that was the end of the inning.

Back in the dugout after everybody had given him a thump or two by way of congratulations, his coach took Coco aside. "Maybe you could have struck out your brother instead of walking a run home?" he said.

"No way," said Coco. "I can't throw anything that he can't hit."

"Well it was good thinking," said the coach. "But it took a lot of nerve. You couldn't be sure of getting the other three batters."

"I could be surer of getting them than I could of getting Rory," said Coco.

"He doesn't look like such a good hitter to me," said the coach.

"He's been hitting me for years," said Coco. "You wait. When he catches on, he can hit anybody."

In the next inning, with the Yankees at bat, two men struck out in quick succession and a third got on with a little blooper that went over the pitcher's head and was missed by the shortstop.

It was now Coco's turn to bat. Ever since the start

of the baseball season, he had been saying to himself "choke up" when he went to bat, but he took two swings at ridiculous pitches with his grip on the end of the bat before his own message got through to him. Then he choked up and the next two pitches were balls, leaving the count two and two. The third was a little low and on the outside corner of the plate, but he swung at it anyway. He felt a solid thump as the bat connected and started for first with a quick glance at the ball. It was soaring way out to center field, seemingly still climbing. He headed for second without slacking his pace. He was rounding second and headed for third when he heard a cheer from the stands and, turning, saw his brother Rory in center field with the ball in his hand. He had caught it just as it was going to clear the fence.

"Why did you try so hard?" demanded Coco after the game, which the Yankees won 5–2. "Gosh, you could have just missed it and let me have my home run."

"Why did you walk me with the bases loaded?" asked Rory. "You're lucky to be alive. What was that last pitch you threw when you struck out Stammers?"

"I didn't really throw it," said Coco.

"What do you mean you didn't really throw it? You were out there on the mound."

"Well, it was kind of like Kevin threw it," said

Coco. "I went into my stretch and remembered Kevin saying not to try to throw so hard. So I took something off the ball, and it kind of floated down to the plate. It wasn't turning very much. Sort of a knuckle ball."

"From where I was standing on first, it looked like it was wobbling," said Rory.

"It was a Krazy Kevin pitch," said Coco. "I'll never be able to throw it again in a million years."

"Oh yes you will," said Rory. "We'll work on it. It might be a real winner."

Chapter Eight

A few days later there was a meeting of the White's Beach Baseball Committee. It was the first meeting Mr. Hurley had been able to attend since his election —or railroading, as he preferred to call it. The chairman was the contractor Al Flint, and the other members present were Dottie Green, who was chairman of the ladies' auxiliary, Chuck Waller, a certified public accountant, and Ed Sullivan, who handled several accounts for Webber, Winstrom and Kurt, a big advertising agency.

At the meeting Mr. Hurley was called on for a report on the progress of the Pancake Breakfast, and he said he had made arrangements for the use of the Recreation Hall, the tickets were being printed, he'd located forty folding chairs and three long tables but needed many more, and the bakery had agreed to mix the pancake mix.

"We're going to use paper plates to save washing up, and I've got a promise of a gross of knives and forks and spoons through the ladies' auxiliary," he said. "I've also been promised four gas-fired grills for cooking. I guess you can say it's going all right. But there are so many odds and ends to attend to, I won't know until the day comes. I'll need lots of volunteer helpers."

"You'll get them," said Al Flint. "When can we have the tickets?"

"Monday next—but somebody has to write a check for them."

"Let me have the bill in triplicate and it will be paid in due course," said the accountant, primly.

"It's going to have to be paid faster than due course," said Mr. Hurley. "The printer's very busy and he didn't need the business. He printed the tickets as a personal favor, and it's going to be too bad if we keep him hanging around for his money."

"It will be paid," said Mr. Flint, who was plainly a man who got things done his way. "Just let him send a bill."

"In triplicate," said the accountant.

"You can make two copies," said Flint. "What's next?"

"It would be nice if we got an important personage to agree to attend the Pancake Breakfast as a sort of a draw," said Mr. Sullivan smoothly. "Might get a lot more people to turn out that way."

"That's a good idea," said Mrs. Green, and Waller, the accountant, agreed.

"Who had you got in mind?" asked Mr. Hurley. "Willie Davis or Hank Aaron? Some ballplayer?"

"No. The season's started and they're hard to get hold of. Their schedule is too tough, anyway, and we're too small."

"Well, who?" said Mr. Hurley. "Lorne Green? He lives out here some place."

Mr. Sullivan smiled. "Mr. Green's a very nice man," he said, "but I'm sure he's pretty busy. How about Joe Soderstrom. This was part of his district when he was in the Congress."

"Isn't he running for Congress again?" asked Mr. Hurley.

"Yes. That's correct."

"Uh-uh," said Mr. Hurley. "That just smells a little bit too political to me."

"Now just a minute," said Sullivan. "If the Governor of California came to the Pancake Breakfast, you wouldn't throw him out—would you? So why not Joe Soderstrom? I'm pretty sure I could arrange some television coverage too." And looking across at Mr. Hurley, Mr. Sullivan added, with a smile, "Publicity's the name of the game."

"Uh-uh," said Mr. Hurley. "Baseball's the name of the game."

He was irritated about the whole thing and complained to Al Flint afterward. "That's what's wrong with the whole country right now," he said. "Everything's being exploited for some other end. Isn't there just one thing left in the nation that can be just what it says it is and nothing more—nothing hidden?"

"You ever played on a teeter-totter when you were a kid?" asked Al.

"Sure. But what's that got to do with it?"

"Well, everything's like that," said Al Flint. "It takes two to make things work. One goes down and the other goes up. Then it's reversed. The down goes up, and the up goes down. Nothing works in isolation."

"This isn't teeter-totter," said Mr. Hurley. "It's kids' baseball. And it should be kept clean of politicking."

"Someday we may need a favor," said Al. "It's nice to have friends when you need something."

"Bah," said Mr. Hurley. "I'm not working on this Pancake Breakfast to give some candidate a platform on which to stand."

Al said nothing for a while. Then he surprised Mr. Hurley with a request. "When you have the tickets printed, give me a hundred," he said.

"You can sell a hundred tickets—just like that?"

"Maybe more," said Al.

"Who to?"

"Just give me the tickets—one goes up, the other goes down. Remember?"

Mr. Hurley went home annoyed and depressed.

"It's the principle of the thing," he said to his wife. "Baseball's for baseball—not for getting elected." But in the days that followed he discovered that very few people cared about the principle. What they were concerned about was how many tickets were sold. And there was no doubt that the publicity the event received from the announcement that Soderstrom was to be present sold tickets.

The announcements weren't much. Just one-line statements—mentioning that Soderstrom would be present at the Pancake Breakfast in aid of the White's Beach Junior Baseball Program, April 10—attached to another story. They made Soderstrom look good and they brought the event to the attention of many who would never have heard of it. The advance ticket sale ran into several hundred, and Mr. Hurley began to wonder whether he had ordered enough pancake flour and syrup and sausages.

"If you run out," said Mr. Heinz, the baker, "let me know. I've got flour and eggs and milk I can let you have. You can replace them later."

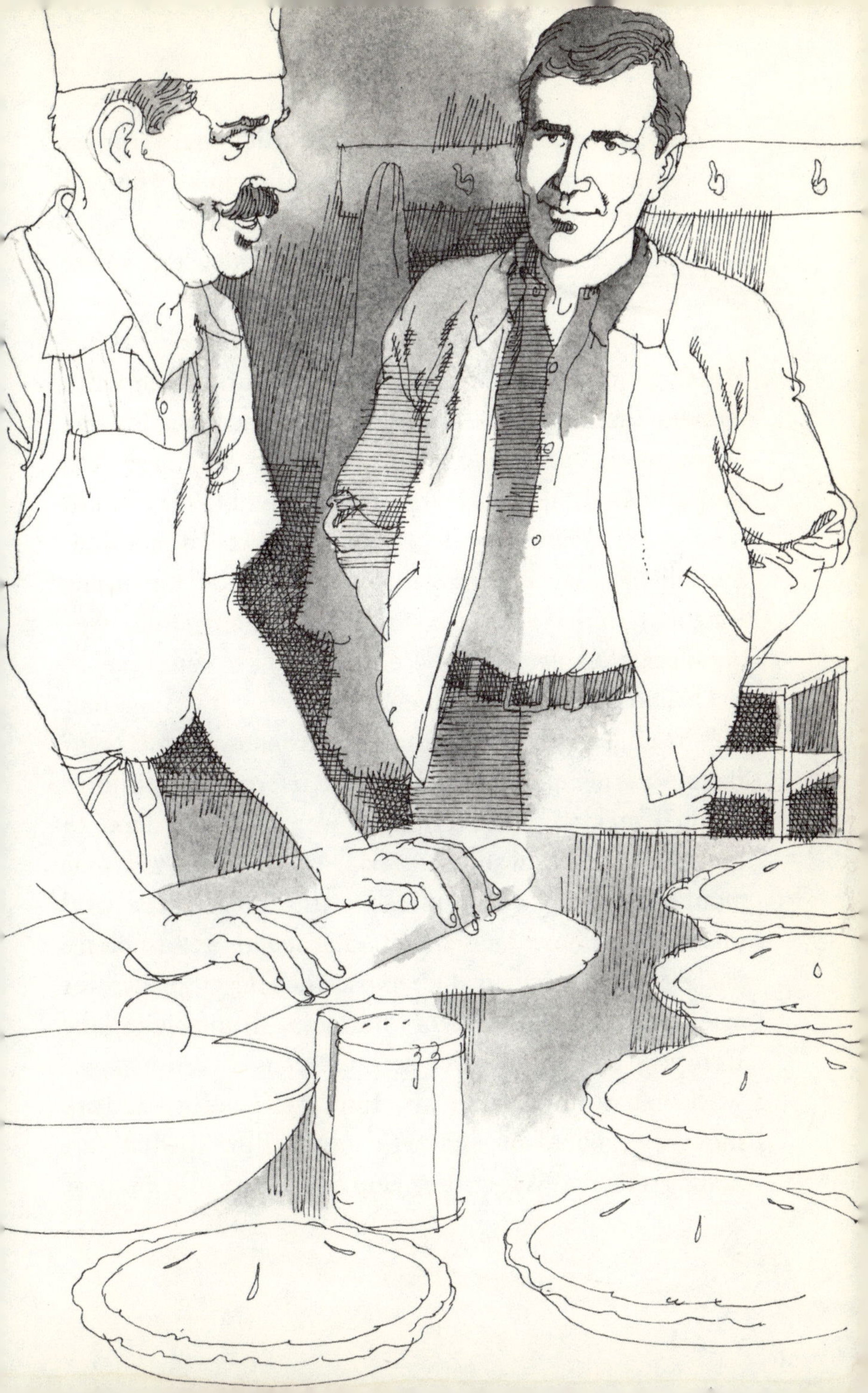

"Anytime you need a friend," said Mr. Hurley, "you've got one. We're printing an announcement that you mixed everything up for us on our bulletin, but I know that isn't really compensation for what you're doing."

This conversation took place in Mr. Heinz's bakery. He was getting some pies ready to put in the oven later in the day. "No, the announcement won't do me much good, though I thank you for it," said Mr. Heinz. "I'm not doing it for that reason. I've lived here twenty-eight years. People have been good to me, all in all. It's my town. I'm glad to do something for it."

"We ought to have more people like you in politics," said Mr. Hurley.

"Uh-uh," said Mr. Heinz. "You know something? People blame politicians for what is really their own fault. The kind of government we get is the kind of government we want, by and large. Otherwise we wouldn't put up with it. It's like this bakery. The kind of bread and pies and doughnuts people get from me is the kind they want. Otherwise they'd go somewhere else, and I'd be out of business. Same with the Congress and so on. Congressmen can't run things the way they want or they wouldn't get re-elected. Like me they got to produce the goods the people are willing to buy. When they don't, it's basically because the people don't care. And if they don't care, they're not being hurt, are they?"

"Well, there's something to think about," said Mr. Hurley.

Heinz, stirring a mixture of batter in a bowl gave him a quick look. "You're sore about Soderstrom coming to the breakfast, I hear," he said.

"Yes, I am. I don't see how you can mix politics with kids' baseball."

"Well, you're mixing my bakery with kids' baseball, aren't you? I give you something. You accept it and publicize me. He gives you something, what's wrong with accepting it and publicizing him?"

"I don't know. It just seems wrong," said Mr. Hurley.

"You ought to think about it," said Mr. Heinz. "Politicians perform services just like bakers. No sense being down on them just because they're politicians. Heard you were short of chairs. They must have a raft of them down at Soderstrom's election headquarters in L.A. No reason why you couldn't ask him for some. You mind my asking how old you are?"

"Pushing forty," said Mr. Hurley.

"Tell you something," said Mr. Heinz. "I was forty before I made the most important discovery in my life."

"What was that?" asked Mr. Hurley.

"I'll tell you for free," said the baker. "When you meet someone new, you can either make a friend or an enemy. Friends are better than enemies, so why not make friends? It isn't much when you put it in words. But it has sure made a lot of difference in my life. That and learning how to cut angel food cake."

"How do you cut angel food cake?" asked Mr. Hurley.

"Wet the serrated knife in hot water first," said the baker.

Chapter Nine

Two days before the Pancake Breakfast, when Mr. Hurley was in the final stages of rounding up what seemed sufficient supplies to feed a division of the Army, Mr. Pestinock called him into his office.

"You're taking your eye off the ball, Hurley. You're beginning to slip," he said. "There's only one way to work for this company, and that's all the time. You're slacking off."

Mr. Hurley had learned from experience that it was best to say nothing to the opening condemnations of his boss. "You know what I'm talking about," Mr. Pestinock went on. "That coffee opportunity in Hawaii. You initiated that thing. You got it going. I warned you about the competition getting into the nest and stealing the eggs. And that's just what they've done. I had a call last night from Ed Jenkins. You know who he is—export manager at Catchall Container Corporation."

"He said would I like to play golf Saturday, and they have an order for ten thousand containers from the Kona coffee people. You see what I mean? You did the spadework, and they reaped the harvest. Now I'm going to take a big chance on you. I'm going to send you to Hawaii right now, and I'm going to expect you to talk the coffee growers out of that order or at least give us a similar order at the same price. You plane leaves in an hour. Have your wife bring you a bag to the airport. There isn't time for you to go home."

"Tomorrow's Friday," said Mr. Hurley. "Can't this wait until Monday? I can't get much done on a Friday. With the weekend ahead most people will be away from their offices early."

"Friday or not, I want you over there right now," said Mr. Pestinock. "That's the trouble with you, Hurley. You're losing your hustle. Now pull yourself together and get with it."

"Boss," said Mr. Hurley, "I'm sure I can do whatever can be done on Monday. I could take a plane Sunday night and be there ready to get busy first thing Monday morning. Besides I have an obligation to attend to here Saturday, that I just can't get out of like that."

"An obligation?" said Mr. Pestinock. "What kind of an obligation?"

"It's a pancake breakfast," said Mr. Hurley.

"A what?"

"A pancake breakfast. I have been put in charge of the Pancake Breakfast for the Junior Baseball program in White's Beach on Saturday, and I have to be there."

"Have you gone out of your mind?" said Mr. Pestinock. "We're talking about winning or losing a big new account, maybe running into hundreds of thousands of dollars annually for this company in the years ahead, and you come up mumbling about a pancake breakfast. What's got into you, Hurley?"

"Boss," said Mr. Hurley, "I didn't volunteer for this Pancake Breakfast. I was railroaded into it. I've been working on it for a long time now. There's a heck of a lot to organizing a pancake breakfast, starting from scratch. Anyway, I'm in charge. It comes off on Saturday. And I just can't be in Hawaii when it comes off because the whole thing will collapse, and I have to go on living in White's Beach."

"Then get someone else to take over for you," said Mr. Pestinock. "And don't miss that plane to Hawaii."

"I'll see what I can do," said Mr. Hurley and went back to his office. He was lucky and got Al Flint on the phone at the first try and explained the situation.

"It wouldn't be so bad if we didn't have Soderstrom coming," said Al. "Too bad if the breakfast wound up a mess with him there and the television people too. Make the whole city look sick."

"Al," said Mr. Hurley, "this is a matter of business. Can you really ask me to put that Pancake Breakfast ahead of my job?"

"Matter of values," said Al, who was an expert at twisting arms. "There are a lot of people looking forward to this event . . ."

"Look here," said Mr. Hurley, "you got me into this thing. Now you get me out of it."

"I guess I could take over myself," said Al dubiously. "I was planning on coming down and giving a hand. Of course, I've got that condominium to the point where I ought to get to it and see if the plumbers turn up, otherwise I'm going to be wasting wages, and I had to estimate that job down to the last dime. And I got a green crew digging trenches for forms . . ."

"Well, somebody has got to take over because I have to go to Hawaii," said Mr. Hurley.

He tidied up his desk, answered some questions

that his secretary put to him about matters that would come up in his absence, and drove to the airport. At the Polynesian Airways counter he met his wife with a weekend bag.

"It's go or be fired," he said gloomily. "And that may shoot the Pancake Breakfast clean out of the sky. You know most of the details—Heinz to mix the batter; flour and sausages stored at the Better Food Market—call Tom Winter the manager and he'll get them for you. The pancake mix has to be at Heinz's at four in the morning for preparation. There are three gas burners at the Recreation Hall and the fourth is still at the Center Street School . . ."

"Darling," said his wife, "don't worry. We'll get it all together somehow if we have to. But I have a better idea."

"What's that?"

"The Pancake Breakfast is Saturday morning. Right? So why not take a night flight back from Hawaii and you can be here to handle everything. It's only six hours' flying time. You could leave at six in the evening, which is nine our time and be here at three in the morning and ready to go to work. You could sleep on the plane."

"Fly two thousand miles for a kids' Pancake Breakfast?" said Mr. Hurley. "That's ridiculous."

"Is a kids' Pancake Breakfast really such a small thing?" asked his wife. Mr. Hurley examined her in silence for a while.

"Every now and then," he said, "I realize all over again why I married you. I'll do it. Just get the groceries and everything into the Recreation Hall. There's a list of where everything is to come from and how it is to be picked up on my desk. I'll be there—by dawn's early light."

On the plane, feeling somewhat flustered, he gave the stewardess a book of tickets to the breakfast instead of his flight coupon. She looked them over with a slight smile and asked, "These for sale?"

"Yes," said Mr. Hurley.

"I'll see what I can do," she said, and having checked his flight coupon went off. Mr. Hurley settled down and slept most of the way to Hawaii. There wasn't much to occupy him—just clouds and the faint hum of the plane which he found soothing. When they reached Honolulu the stewardess gave him six dollars.

"We're all coming back tomorrow—the night flight," she said. "We usually get breakfast at the airport. But it would be fun to have a pancake breakfast instead."

"You mean the whole crew of the plane?"

"The whole crew. Hope the pancakes are good."

"So do I," said Mr. Hurley.

The following morning, Friday, having made arrangements to take a night flight back to Los Angeles, Mr. Hurley called on the Kona Coffee Growers Organization. He called at eight in the morning, but no one answered. He called at nine, but nobody of importance was yet at work. He decided to go over to the head office, located in a suite in one of the big hotels on the waterfront by Waikiki. He sat there until eleven before the receptionist told him that Mr. Carson, the purchasing agent, whom he hoped to see, had phoned to say he was not coming in but had to leave for the big island of Hawaii and his assistant couldn't see Hurley until Monday. Mr. Hurley reflected for a moment and called Mr. Li of the orchid growers, who was the only person in Honolulu whom he could claim to know.

Mr. Li had left for lunch but his secretary thought that if it was important Mr. Hurley might find him at the Royal Hawaiian in the Hibiscus Room. Mr. Li was there with several other gentlemen, and Mr. Hurley was dubious about disturbing him. But the headwaiter, having announced his presence, beckoned him over to the table and Mr. Hurley went over and said, "I just dropped by to say hello. Don't let me interfere, please."

"Sit down, sit down," said Mr. Li. "My friends and I were just talking about a round of golf. You have time?"

Mr. Hurley hesitated. "I have to try to get hold of some people at the Kona Coffee Growers Organization," he said, and explained briefly. Mr. Li shook his head.

"The gentlemen you probably should see are not here," he said. "Friday is not a good day for business meetings. Why not a weekend of golf—starting this afternoon?"

"Not a weekend," said Mr. Hurley. "I have to get a night plane back to California."

"Mr. Hurley doesn't really like Hawaii," said Mr. Li sadly to his companions.

"Oh no," said Mr. Hurley. "I love Hawaii. I have to get back for—a special occasion."

"A wedding anniversary?" asked Mr. Li.

"No."

"A birthday?"

"No. A pancake breakfast."

"A pancake breakfast?" said Mr. Li. "Two thousand miles for a pancake breakfast? They must be very good pancakes."

"They will probably be the worst pancakes that were ever cooked, but I have to be there," said Mr. Hurley and explained the situation. They all listened in mild surprise and Mr. Hurley left.

Mr. Hurley made two further attempts to make contact with the coffee growers, but without success. He regretfully concluded that nothing could be done until Monday morning and, but for Mr. Pestinock's impatience, he might well have remained in California. In short, he had wasted time and money in flying to Hawaii. He caught the plane back to Los Angeles feeling depressed and aware that he would have to pay the fare to California and back out of his own pocket. He wondered whether Mr. Pestinock wasn't right after all. Maybe he really was losing his sense of proportion and neglecting business for outside activity.

Chapter Ten

Mr. Hurley got back to Los Angeles a little after three in the morning. He had scarcely slept on the plane from Honolulu and his eyes felt as if they were loaded with hot sand. His clothes didn't seem to fit anymore, his mouth was dry and as he drove to his home in White's Beach he wondered how he was going to get through the next hour, let alone the whole long day ahead. At home his wife said he ought to lie down for an hour and she would wake him at four-thirty. So he lay down and slept until quarter past five, woke in a panic, threw his clothes on, washed and dashed down to the Heinz Bakery.

Mr. Heinz shook his head when he let him in through the backdoor. "You'd never make a baker," he said. "Where's the pancake mix?"

"They didn't get it to you?"

"Uh-uh. It's probably still at the grocery. And that's shut. But don't panic. I've mixed up a couple of gallons here to get you started out of my own stuff. Take it on down to the Recreation Hall, and bring back the rest from the grocery."

That was just the start of the day's crises. Mr. Hurley called the grocer and a sleepy voice told him that the grocer had gone away for the weekend fishing. He explained about the pancake mix and the other groceries which should have been collected the evening before, and the grocer's wife (it was she who had answered the telephone) said she'd send her son down in an hour to get the stuff for him.

"I've got to have it right away—an hour won't do," said Mr. Hurley. But her son had driven his father down to nearby San Pedro to go out on a boat for the day's fishing and wouldn't be back for an hour. Mr. Hurley called his wife. "This is going to cost us every friend we have in the world," he said. "But call all the neighbors and get all the boxes of pancake mix they have and get them over to the Heinz Bakery. Somebody goofed and didn't get the supplies from the grocery."

"You mean call them at five-thirty on a Saturday morning when everybody's sleeping in?" said Mrs. Hurley.

"Right," said her husband. "Next week we can sell

the house and move to another city. Send those two sons of mine down here. They're the cause of all this."

This utterly unjust accusation made Mr. Hurley feel a lot better. One or two volunteer helpers had turned up and luckily the paper plates and cutlery were on hand. But nobody had bothered to set out the chairs and the tables the night before, and when Rory and Coco arrived they were told to do this. Mrs. Green, however, turned up with two boxes of pancake mix, a large roll of tickets and a cash box. "How come you didn't get the groceries down to the baker?" she asked, rather smugly, giving Mr. Hurley the boxes of pancake mix.

"Because I was in Hawaii," said Mr. Hurley.

"What did you go there for?" asked Mrs. Green. "Surely you knew that the Pancake Breakfast was today."

"Because I love surfing," said Mr. Hurley, grimly.

One of the volunteers came up. "Where's the paper napkins?" he asked. "There's no paper napkins."

"They're somewhere," said Mr. Hurley. "They were with the plates."

"Can't find them."

"Have another look. They must be around."

"What about trash barrels?" said another. "Where do we put all the used paper plates and garbage and stuff?"

"Aren't there trash barrels outside?"

"Nope. Just this small one right here in the kitchen."

"I'll call Tony," said Mr. Hurley.

Tony was the groundsman and janitor for the Recreation Department. The trash barrels were stored in a small room in the back of the building. "Got to keep them locked up all the time," said Tony. "The way people steal is getting to be something awful these days. Would you ever figure on people stealing trash barrels—I mean right here in America?"

"Tony," said Mr. Hurley. "I wouldn't. But would you mind coming down here and getting them out. Because if we don't get those trash barrels in an hour or so this whole place is going to be littered with old paper plates covered with pancake syrup."

"Should be some way to save those paper plates," said Tony. "I mean it's ecology. Like if . . ."

"Tony," said Mr. Hurley. "Please!"

"Okay," said Tony. "I'll get down there. Take about an hour though. That car of mine . . ."

Mr. Hurley hung up and saw Rory standing by him. "Tell me some good news," he said. "Otherwise don't say a word."

"Two of the ranges are working swell," said Rory, cheerfully.

"Two," cried Mr. Hurley. "What happened to the other two? There were supposed to be four."

"There isn't a connecting thing for one of them, and the other is electric and they've lost the cord."

"It's okay," said someone. "I've found the cord. Hey, look out the door there—dawn."

"Hey, look at the door there," echoed Coco. "People."

And so there were, a line of people, which was getting longer by the moment. Mr. Hurley glanced at the clock. It was a quarter to seven. He suddenly remembered coffee.

"Did anybody make coffee?" he asked.

"That's a dumb question," said one of the volunteers cheerfully. "The first thing anybody makes in this country is coffee. We've got ten gallons. But no orange juice. And no milk."

"I'll be back," said Mr. Hurley.

"Where are you going?" asked Mrs. Green as he passed.

"I'm going to kick the door out of that grocery store," said Mr. Hurley.

"Oh, I thought you might be going to Hawaii again."

But when he got to the grocery he found the grocer's son already there. Mr. Hurley loaded twenty half pints of milk into the back of his car and the same number of orange juice and flew back to the Recreation Hall with them.

He was just in time to serve the first group of children who arrived with their parents. He spent the next hour and a half on a sort of ferrying service, bringing milk and orange juice from the grocery and mixed pancake batter from the bakery. In between times he dealt with the garbage problem momentarily by having the help stack the plates and stuff them in brown paper grocery bags of which his wife (and several other wives) had an astonishing supply.

But the collecting and stacking of the plates slowed the service down and this problem wasn't relieved until Tony got the trash cans out of the storeroom. Several boys had now turned up, and they were put to the job of cleaning off the tables and taking orders.

By nine o'clock the line outside was a block long and Mr. Hurley discovered that some people were waiting twenty minutes before getting breakfast. So instead of having the people come in, be seated, and then be served by the boys, he started cafeteria service—pancakes on plates with sausages at one end of a counter and pancakes on plates without sausages at the other end of the counter. Milk and orange juice were put on a table for people to help themselves, and the boys went around with coffee served in styrofoam cups. This speeded things up considerably, and by nine-thirty Mr. Hurley was able to stop ferrying and looking for stuff and relieve one of the men who had been cooking pancakes for two solid hours.

"How's it going?" he asked as he took over.

"Good," said the other. "Hey. Don't make them so big. Big 'uns take longer to cook, and people don't like to eat hot blankets."

Mr. Hurley quickly found that cooking pancakes took some kind of knack which he didn't possess.

"Mind if I give you a tip?" asked the man beside him working briskly away.

"Nope," said Mr. Hurley. "Glad of it."

"You're wasting half the hotplate," said the man. "Just put little pancakes in rows using every square inch you can. Pour the batter up on the hotplate in the space nearest you first, then work up and down. That way you know those nearest you are always cooked first. And you can clear the hotplate quicker."

He stuck it out for an hour with medium success and then Al Flint turned up. "Got my crew going," he said. "I'll take over. What time did you get back from Hawaii?"

"Just after the Fall of Rome," said Mr. Hurley. "Three o'clock this morning actually."

The man who had been helping him looked up. "You came back from Hawaii to be here?" he asked.

"Yes," said Mr. Hurley. "I'm supposed to be in charge."

"I didn't get your name," said the man.

"Hurley. Pete Hurley."

"Pleased to meet you, Mr. Hurley. I'm Joe Soderstrom."

"Joe Soderstrom? You mean the former congressman?"

"Right."

"But I thought you were going to come down and just have breakfast and be photographed," said Mr. Hurley.

"So I was. But when I got here, it looked like you needed some help in the kitchen."

"TV crew should be here any minute," said Al Flint. "How do I look?"

Soderstrom grinned. "Al," he said. "You're the oldest fox in the business. Made my boys buy two hundred tickets, and now you're getting in on the action."

"Joe," said Al. "The only business that's good business is when there's something in it for everybody."

Al Flint had indeed timed his own arrival perfectly. A few minutes later the cameramen arrived from the TV station and took some film of Soderstrom cooking pancakes with Al Flint and Mr. Hurley in the background and Soderstrom serving some of the young players with pancakes.

Mr. Hurley watched all this with mixed feelings. He couldn't deny that the attendance at the breakfast had been the heavier for Soderstrom's presence. He couldn't deny that the TV publicity would help Junior Baseball in White's Beach and elsewhere. He still felt, however, that it was dangerous to mix a Junior Baseball program up with political maneuvers.

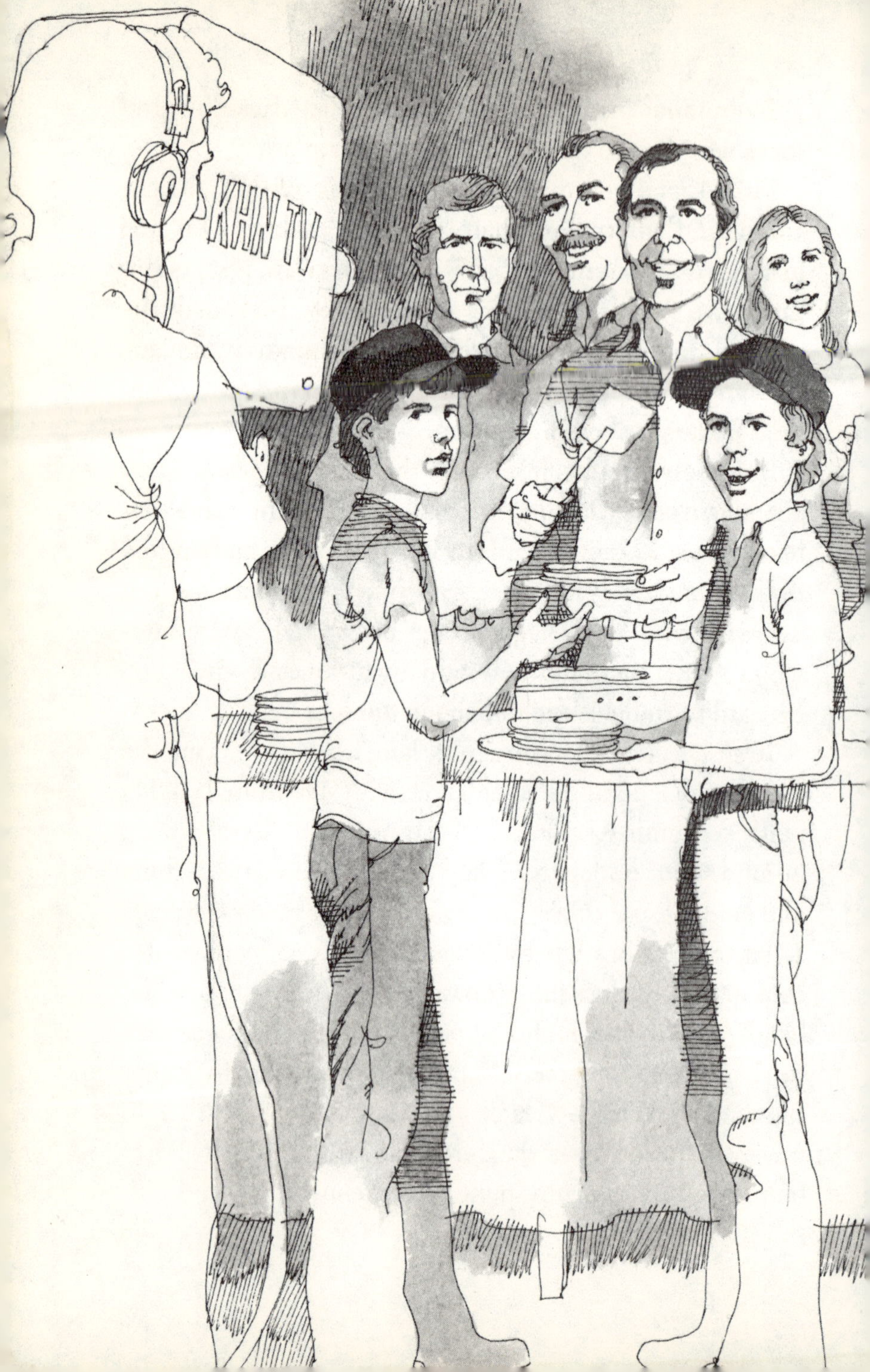
KHN TV

By midmorning the crowd began to dwindle, and there was time to take stock and clean up a bit.

Mrs. Green, examining the numbers of her tickets, announced that they had served breakfast to just under five thousand people, and taken in just under thirty-five hundred dollars. Mr. Hurley reckoned the cost of the groceries roughly at six hundred dollars, meaning a profit on paper of two thousand nine hundred dollars.

But these figures lumbered through his head without leaving any lasting impression. The hot sand was back in his eyes and his feet felt as if they had turned to lead. His back hurt and every now and then he felt hot and cold flashes going up his spine. Mr. Soderstrom shook his hand and said good-by and gave him his card with his home telephone number on it.

"Call me if you have a problem," he said. "You did a swell job. Came back from Hawaii, eh? Well. That's really something."

Mr. Hurley thanked him, and Al Flint came over and said, "Why don't you sit down and rest your feet? Everything went great. There's plenty of helpers to take care of the cleaning up."

So Mr. Hurley found an easy chair out of the way in the janitor's quarters, sat down in it, and promptly fell asleep.

Chapter Eleven

Meanwhile the baseball season in White's Beach really settled down to business with games every night of the week and a double-header on Saturdays. Rory's team, the Indians, established an early lead and held onto it largely because they had excellent hitting. The nearest rival were the Yankees, whose pitching staff, headed by Spider Edwards, was the best in the League, largely because he was extremely accurate.

Despite all the coaching that his elder brothers, Kevin and Rory, gave him, Coco still threw a wild pitch every now and again when called in to relieve. Since he was rarely called in to relieve unless there was no other pitcher available and the bases were loaded, a wild pitch was costly. More often than not it meant a run.

"Coco," said Kevin, "it's just nerves. You've just got to get hold of yourself. Remember it's only a game."

"That's what I keep telling myself," said Coco. "All the way in from center field, when they call me in to pitch, I keep telling myself it's only a game. Trouble is, I don't believe it."

"But it *is* only a game," said Kevin. "Heck, win or lose, life still goes on."

"It goes on much happier when I win," said Coco. "I don't know what happens with those wild pitches. The ball just gets away from me."

"You try to throw too hard," said Rory. "That's what happens."

"Got to throw hard," said Coco. "With bases loaded who can throw a nice medium ball right down the middle?"

"Look," said Kevin. "In a bases-loaded situation a wild pitch means a sure run. If you throw a strike and the batter connects with a fly ball—even a long fly ball—the man on third has got to tag up. So you have a chance of getting him. And even if you don't get him and he scores, there's one out. And if you throw a strike low—which is the thing to do with bases loaded—even if the batter hits it, it's likely to be a ground ball to the infield and maybe a double play."

"I know that," said Coco. "Everybody knows that. The only thing is that the ball doesn't know that. It's either in the dirt for a passed ball and a run scoring, or its so high it goes to the backstop and the run scores anyway."

Rory thought about this for a while. "You're just too afraid of getting hit with bases loaded," he said. "You forget that there are seven other guys out there—four of them around you in the infield—ready to make an out. I just wish I could catch you. That would solve the whole problem."

"How would it solve the whole problem?" demanded Kevin.

"First wild pitch he threw I'd go right out there to the mound and punch him on the nose," said Rory.

"Better practice some more," said Kevin.

They did, but somehow the practice didn't seem to help. In the driveway by their house, Coco had great control. In a bases-loaded situation, when he was called in because there wasn't another pitcher available, the prospects were that he would throw the ball in the dirt and a run would score. Another trouble was that the Yankee catcher, Cy Strange, spent what time he had catching the first- and second-string pitchers, who were still Spider Edwards and Chuck Podranski. The third baseman, Jackie Green, was the alternate catcher, but he was too busy to work with Coco.

Coco did, however, manage to get some control

over what he called his Krazy Kevin pitch. It wasn't exactly a knuckle ball, though it had a tendency to dance about. For one thing, it revolved slowly, whereas a knuckle ball has no spin or very little spin. In addition, it revolved the reverse way of a regular pitch, which meant that it was much more likely to pop up for an infield out if it were hit. But the oddest thing was that it seemed to drop halfway to the plate and then float up again, so either the batter swung low or didn't swing at all when the ball floated right through the center of the strike zone. But Coco could never be absolutely sure of throwing it. When Kevin learned about it, he advised Coco to forget it.

"If you want to be good," he said, "throw the pitches you know you can throw. Magic never works when you need it. When it comes to luck, the other guy is always likely to have more than you."

"Yeah, but someday I'm going to be the other guy," said Coco.

Meanwhile, Rory was still kept at center field. The alternate catcher on the Indians was the second baseman, Stammers, and Rory never got a chance in the catcher's spot.

The last-place team was the Pirates. They were just a little less efficient in pitching and fielding than the others. They had better hitters, but they lost most of their games on fielding errors—long fly balls the outfield should have got to but didn't, and grounders poked past the infield that should have been outs. It was the beginning of June before the cellar-dwelling Pirates made their first double play, and then it was a fluke. The batter hit a short fly ball toward first base. The first baseman caught it and got to the bag before the runner, who had taken a generous lead, could get back, and that was it. It didn't matter much because the Pirates were down 7–2 at the top of the fifth.

They lost the game, and yet that double play produced a subtle change in the team. Everybody on the Pirates had had the feeling that somehow no matter what they did, they couldn't win. Now they began to feel that the breaks didn't have to be against them all the time. They won the next two games, against the Orioles and the top-place Indians, and though they lost to the Yankees, it took extra innings before they went down.

"After the rain comes the sunshine," said the Pirate coach, and people who had been feeling a little sorry for the team now began to be a little nervous about them. Perhaps it was that the Pirates had at last begun to learn from their own fielding errors—learn lessons the coach had been unable to teach them however hard he tried. But the day came when the Pirates passed the Orioles and were challenging the Yankees for second place, being but half a game out.

"It's our turn to win and their turn to lose," said the Pirate coach. "Just keep playing the way you are. When you come up to bat, I'm going to give you a lot of signals, but don't take any notice of any of them unless I call you over and tell you different. I want you to hit anything that looks good—inside, outside, high, or low."

"We may miss a lot of walks," said the team captain.

"Concentrate on hits and the heck with the walks," said the coach. "When you're at bat you're on offense, not defense. Think offense."

The Pirates took that advice to heart, and in the critical game with the Indians did so well that at the top of the sixth the game was tied three all. The Pirates were at bat with one out and the lead run at third. Up came Dusty Martin, the star Pirate hitter. He was big and round. His shoulders were sloped and he looked unco-ordinated, but for all that he led the team in hits, batting around .320. The pitcher watched him shuffle the dirt in the batter's box around with his cleats and threw the ball a couple of times into his glove. That was the signal for a curve low and on the outside corner.

That is what the pitcher threw and Dusty Martin swung because he had been told to swing at anything he liked. He liked low balls. He connected and pulled the ball to left field. It wasn't a good clean hit. The ball was spinning wildly when it hit the ground in foul territory short of third base. It bounded immediately back in, making it a fair ball. The runner on third had taken off with the pitch. The third baseman caught the ball and fired to home plate. Al Harter, the catcher, got the ball just as the runner came thundering in. Catcher and runner tangled in a melee of dust and flying arms and legs. The runner got to the plate, and the ball was knocked from Al's hand and trickled toward the backstop. Al lay on the ground for a moment and then got up slowly nursing his left hand. The Indian coach ran out to him and took a look at it. Already the hand was beginning to swell.

"See if you can bend your fingers," said the coach. Al tried, grimacing, and succeeded.

"Good," said the coach. "No bones broken. But you'll have to come out." He looked about. Stammers, the second baseman was the relief catcher. But he didn't have a good second baseman in the dugout, and the way the Pirates were hitting, any weakness there would mean a lot of runs and lost outs.

He conferred with the pitcher and the first baseman and signaled to Rory in the outfield.

"You're catching," he said, when Rory came trotting in. "Get those shin guards on, and make sure you and the pitcher are working on the same signals."

Chapter Twelve

Rory conferred with the pitcher about signals and the game situation before settling down at the plate. The signals were simple. If he put one finger down it meant a fast ball. Two meant a curve; three a change-up. That was about the extent of the pitcher's ability, and it was certainly all that he needed. As for the game situation, the Pirates were a run ahead, there was one out, and they had a man on first.

"Should be easy to pick Dusty off," said Rory. "He runs like a bag of water with a hole in it. How's the umpire?"

"He doesn't like them low," said the pitcher. "Just above the knees is a ball."

"Well, let's get 'em out," said Rory and went back to the plate. He squatted down and the batter stepped into the box. "Real good surf at Paddleboard Creek," said Rory to the batter, signaling for a fast ball.

The batter said nothing. "Want to go down after the game?" asked Rory. The fast ball came in with the batter looking. Strike one. The batter got ready again and the pitcher threw to first—just a toss to drive Dusty back.

"That was a fast ball," said Rory. "I'm signaling for a curve now." He signaled for another fast ball. It came in a little high, but the batter swung and missed.

"You want to shut up?" said the batter turning around to Rory. Rory grinned through his mask. "Only trying to be helpful," he said. "You got two fast balls. It's a cinch you're going to get a change-up now." The batter called for time, and the umpire held up his hand and grinned.

"Take your time," said Rory. "Ease the pressure a little. Gosh a feller don't want to hit into a double play in this situation."

The batter stepped back into the box and Rory squatted down again and put down four fingers—that was an agreed signal for the pitcher to shake his head as if shaking off a sign. They went through that routine twice, to unsettle the batter, and Rory signaled for a change-up. He got a curve ball, high and outside instead, that nearly got away from him. He walked the ball back to the plate. "I called for a change-up," he said.

"That's what I threw," said the pitcher. "But the ball didn't know it."

"Okay," said Rory. "The signal's going to be three fingers—change-up." It was a good change-up that came in right over the strike zone. But the batter had been expecting it. He did little more than just meet it, but he met it fair and the ball fell just short of the charging center fielder who had taken Rory's place. The grass in center field was thick and the ball stopped dead, so the center fielder overcharged it and Dusty Martin loped around second and into third.

Now there was still only one out and a man on third and a man on first. Dusty, on third, wasn't a fast runner but he was famous for scoring by bowling over catchers and knocking the ball out of their gloves, and the Pirate dugout cheered.

"Big inning. Big inning," they shouted. "Everybody hits." The next man walked, loading the bases, and this called for a meeting on the mound.

"How you feeling?" the coach asked the pitcher.

"Good."

"What do you think?" asked the coach, turning to Rory. "How's his control?"

"Okay," said Rory. "Umpire doesn't like 'em low. A couple of those were strikes, but he called them balls."

The infielders came over to join the conference.

"They're only one run ahead," said the coach. "Watch for long fly balls. Dusty isn't much of a runner and you may be able to pick him off at the plate. Just keep pecking away. Don't anybody lose his nerve. Keep calm and play ball."

It seemed, however, that the pitcher had lost his control. His next three pitches were balls, but he recovered with a fast ball right down the middle, which caught the batter looking, and followed this with a change-up at which the batter swung well ahead of the ball. The next pitch was a foul fly ball wide of first base. The first baseman caught it and as soon as he had it in his glove, he was startled to see Dusty Martin take off from third.

The first baseman threw to home plate. It was not a good throw. The ball dropped in the dirt a little in front of Rory who grabbed it and whirled around to meet what seemed like two tons of Dusty Martin coming in at jet speed. They collided inches from the plate, Dusty going over the top of Rory, who lost his mask and got a knee in his nose and part of a boot. But he held onto the ball, and the plate umpire called the runner out.

There was an immediate uproar from the stands, part of the crowd denouncing Dusty for trying to get home, others shouting that the ball had been out of

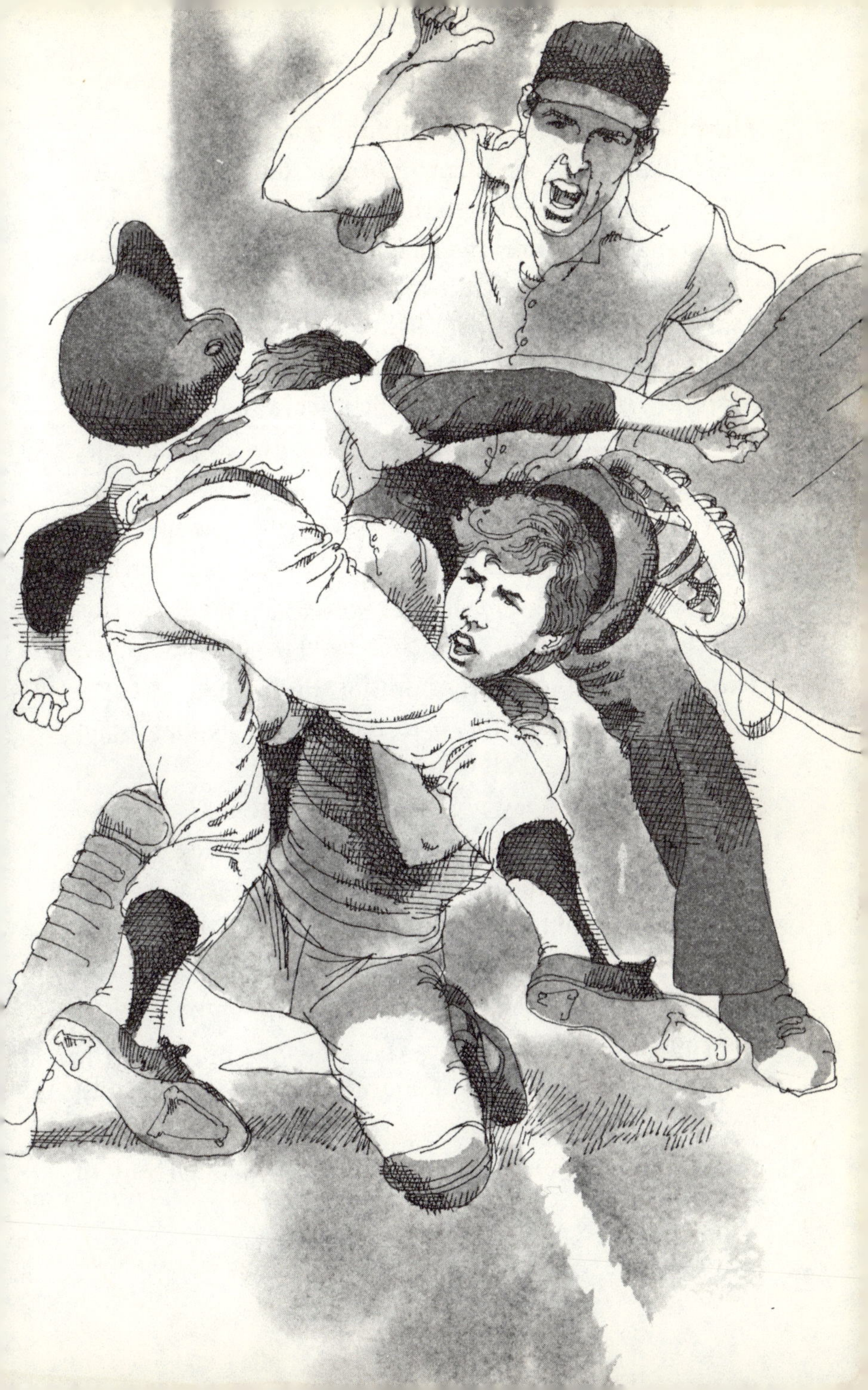

play when caught in foul ground and others yet that the run had scored. But the outcry didn't change the ruling. Both the batter and the runner were out and the side retired. Rory went back to the Indian dugout feeling that his nose and a large part of his face surrounding it had been frozen. He was aware of a general ache in his left shoulder.

"Great work," said the coach. "Feel okay?"

"Yes," said Rory, rubbing his nose. He still had very little feeling in it.

"You're up next," said the coach. "Take your time, though. Stall a little."

Rory took off his gear and selected a bat. He put the doughnut on the end of it and tried a swing or two. His shoulder hurt, but not that much, and he swung the bat around over his head to loosen things up.

The first pitch was a strike at which Rory swung too low and too late. He took on the next two pitches, which were balls, and glancing at the third-base coach caught the signal to take again. He took and had another strike called on him, the count now being two and two.

"This next one is going to be a change-up," said the catcher. Rory grinned. He was being given some of his own medicine. The pitcher stepped onto the rubber and Rory called for time and stepped out of the batting box. He picked up a handful of dirt, rubbed it down the bat and rubbed the rest of it on the seat of his pants.

He glanced at the third-base coach who touched first the black of his hat and then the gray of his uniform, then the black of the letters and again the gray of the uniform. That combination, black to gray, black to gray, meant swing. Back in the box Rory watched the pitcher shake off three signs and figured fast ball. It was fast and down the middle, a direct challenge, and Rory swung.

He'd been expecting a fast ball and he hit it square on the meat of the bat. It cleared the pitcher's upflung arm by a hair, and soared into center field right over the top of second base. Rory headed for first base, touched the bag, and glancing toward the outfield headed for second. The ball went over the center fielder's head for he had come in for it, misjudging it against the bright sky. The center fielder turned his back to the ball, ran a step or two, and whirled around again, and caught the ball. Rory, disgusted, loped back to the dugout.

"Real good hit," said the coach. "Just a little wind to help, and that would have been out."

The next hitter was out on the first ball with a little pop-up at the plate. But the third man got on on a fluke; a shot back to the mound which was deflected toward third base. The third baseman was out of position and got to the ball too late and the runner was aboard. The next batter was walked, and the Pirate dugout decided this was the time to help their pitcher by getting on the hitter. The boy's name was Randy Day, and they ignored the rule about not using a player's name. "Randy Day—Double Play," they shouted.

"Shut your eyes Randy—it's safer."

Randy swung and missed.

Strike one.

"That's it. Don't look and you won't get hurt."

"Swing swing, dingaling."

Randy swung and missed.

Strike two.

It was time for the Indian dugout to help Randy by getting on the pitcher.

"Hey, pitcher—you winding up or having a fit?"

"Get your foot out of your ear."

The next pitch was a change-up. With two fast-ball strikes on him, Randy had been expecting the change-up. He had also decided that the one thing he didn't want to do was hit into a double play. The hit-run sign was on, signaled to Randy and the two base runners from the dugout by someone who kept picking up a handful of dirt and pouring it casually through his fingers on the ground.

The only safe place to hit to avoid the double play was through the hole to the outfield. Randy was no long-ball hitter, so he decided to do what nobody was expecting—bunt with two strikes on him. The bunt worked. It went halfway up the third-base line, trickling toward the foul line.

"Leave it—going foul, going foul," yelled the Indian dugout. The third baseman left it. But it didn't go foul. By the time he realized his mistake everybody was safe, the bases loaded, and only one out.

The situation was too tense now for any more shouting from the dugouts. Anything that went into the outfield was likely to score the man at third, evening the score. The pitcher went into his windup and threw a fast ball—low and outside. The second was low and inside. The catcher went out for a conference.

"Whatever you do, don't put it in the dirt in front of me," he said.

"I got to keep it low," said the pitcher. "If I get it up and he hits a long ball, that's it."

"The ump doesn't like the low ball," said the catcher. "Two-and-O count, so you'd better get them up a bit."

The catcher walked back to plate and signaled for a change-up. The pitch fooled the batter who swung ahead of it. The catcher signaled for the curve ball, but the batter held up and the ball missed the strike zone. Three and one and the bases loaded.

Having missed with the curve ball three times the pitcher decided to challenge the batter and threw a fast ball right down the middle. The batter swung and connected solidly. The ball came right back to the pitcher who caught it and threw to second. The runner on second was off the bag and the second baseman stepped on the bag for the double play. The Pirates were saved for the time being.

As it turned out they just managed to squeak through. There were no more runs on either side and they won by a single run. Rory caught the rest of the game, but had no more at bats. The coach had said nothing more to him about catching, but he felt he had done a good job. He would probably play outfield for the rest of the season, but there was at least a chance that he might be called in to catch in relief, and that was enough for him.

Coco, however, was full of optimism. "Bet you catch for All Stars," he said.

"Oh sure," said Rory. "There's about five other guys all catching, and they're going to pick me even though I've been playing center field all season."

"You'll see," said Coco. "You'll catch in All Stars and I'll pitch, and we'll win the first game about sixteen to nothing—me getting ten strike-outs."

"Sure, sure," said Rory, grinning. "And when we're Dad's age we'll be in the Hall of Fame, and we'll have twin Cadillacs—one marked Rory and one marked Coco. Meantime, you got enough money for a hot dog? I'm hungry."

Chapter Thirteen

Meanwhile Mr. Hurley had gone back to Hawaii and spent two frustrating days trying to get the purchasing manager of the Kona coffee organization to at least give his company the same order for containers as had been given to Catchall. It was no use. The coffee growers were very impressed with the Catchall container and decided to give them all their business for the next two years. This was especially bad since Mr. Hurley pioneered the idea of coffee being put up in styrofoam containers. He pointed out that his company had pioneered the idea and should at least be given a chance to bid on the upcoming order. But the purchasing manager said that the company was satisfied with the Catchall price and bidding would only delay placing of an order and delivery of the containers.

Very depressed, Mr. Hurley went back to his hotel after this interview to find two messages waiting for him. Both added to his gloom. One was to call Mr. Pestinock at the earliest moment, either at the office or at home, irrespective of the hour. The matter was urgent. The other was to call Mr. Li of the orchid growers, whom he didn't want to talk to in his present mood. Since he didn't believe in postponing or ducking trouble, he called Mr. Pestinock first.

"Well," said Mr. Pestinock. "How are you making out? Have you nailed that order down?"

"It's no good," said Mr. Hurley. "Catchall have pulled the rug from under us. They've sewed up the coffee growers for two years. The best we can do is keep studying the situation and take advantage of any breaks that come our way."

"You'd better get back here then—tonight," said Mr. Pestinock. "I have a few things I want to go over with you in the morning." Mr. Hurley didn't ask him what things. He had a pretty good idea of what was likely to be the topic of the meeting.

He called Mr. Li who had been away for a couple of days in Seattle and had now returned to Honolulu.

"Ah, Mr. Hurley," said Mr. Li. "So glad you are still here. Can we lunch together tomorrow? The Silver Surf. I have already made the reservations."

"I have to get back to Los Angeles tonight," said

Mr. Hurley. "Don't say it. It isn't that I don't like Hawaii. But things are not going well. My company is under a lot of pressure, and I have to be there."

"More lost containers?" asked Mr. Li.

"No. But the competition is getting tougher, so we have to pitch in stronger."

"You're a very hard worker," said Mr. Li. "You should take more time for leisure."

"Maybe some day that will be possible," said Mr. Hurley. "But right now I just have to bear down. Please forgive me that I can't come to lunch. I would enjoy it immensely, but it just isn't possible at this time."

"I understand," said Mr. Li. "Tell me. The Pancake Breakfast. Was that a success?"

"Went off fine," said Mr. Hurley. "I think we cleared something over two thousand dollars for the baseball program."

"I'm very glad to hear that. Well, I'll see you the next time you are in Honolulu," said Mr. Li and hung up.

The meeting with Mr. Pestinock the next morning was much worse than Mr. Hurley had feared. He got some idea of how grim it was likely to be beforehand, because everybody at the office was so sympathetic toward him.

"I'll get to the point right away," said Mr. Pestinock. "I'm somewhat less than satisfied with your performance in the past several months. I've been hoping for some kind of an improvement, but I haven't seen it. Basically, I think that you've lost interest in your job. You've got your priorities all mixed up for one thing. Some weeks back, if you'll remember, when I was expecting you to read an important report, you were attending some kids' baseball meeting instead. I had to wait around for you to read the report, and you finally turned it back in saying you either couldn't read it or wouldn't read it.

"Then I send you to Hawaii on a very important order and you let it slip through your fingers while you come back here without a word to anyone to organize a pancake breakfast.

"Well, I've been thinking the matter over and I've decided what you need is a new point of view. A change of perspective. So I'm moving you to Arizona. You'll be in charge of the Arizona and New Mexico territory, and we have a new man coming out from Boston who, when you've shown him around, will take over here in California and Hawaii."

"Mr. Pestinock," said Mr. Hurley, when he had recovered a little from this blow. "My home's in White's Beach. That's going to mean living apart from my family all week, or selling my home. I wish you would take that into consideration."

"I'm aware of what it means," said Mr. Pestinock. "I'm sorry about that. But the company has to come first. That's precisely the perspective that I'm trying to give back to you, Hurley. The company comes first because on the company depends the welfare of your family and everything else. That's the way it's got to be. Turner from Boston will be here on Friday. He'll stay with me over the weekend, and I'll expect you to take him over Monday and start showing him the ropes. I should think that in a couple of weeks, he'll be ready to take over."

"If I move to Arizona, will the company pay any part of my travel expenses?" asked Mr. Hurley.

"Dollar a mile up to a limit of eight hundred dollars. That's the company rule," said Mr. Pestinock.

When he got home that evening Mr. Hurley broke the news to his wife. "If I hadn't gotten mixed up in this baseball business, this probably would never have happened," he said.

"I don't think that's true," said his wife. "It's just some kind of office politics. I'll bet they had this arranged a long time ago and were just waiting for the opportunity to spring it on you."

Mr. Hurley shook his head. "Businesses don't work like that," he said. "Businesses work by having the best man in the best spot. They can't work any other way. They can't afford to play favorites. It's make a profit or go under, and I goofed."

"I think you should just quit," said his wife. "They're not being fair. You've done a lot for the company in the past."

"The past isn't the present, and it's the present that counts," said Mr. Hurley. "It has to be that way."

"No, it doesn't," said his wife. "And if you don't quit, I'll quit for you."

"Darling—you're not thinking of what you're saying. I've got fourteen years in with Safehold. If I quit now, I lose whatever pension I've got coming. We have hospital insurance, health insurance, and profit sharing. I'll lose that. And, furthermore, there's a recession on. Jobs are hard to get. And I'm not young anymore. Over forty in this country is old age, as far as jobs are concerned. So we just have to hang in there and do the best we can. I think we should keep the house—it's an investment anyway. And I should just find some place to stay in Phoenix and come home weekends. Maybe we can work it that way."

"What about me and the children? We'll be alone all week. We'll miss you."

"I'll miss you too. But as Mr. Pestinock says, the job has to come first. Because the family depends upon the job."

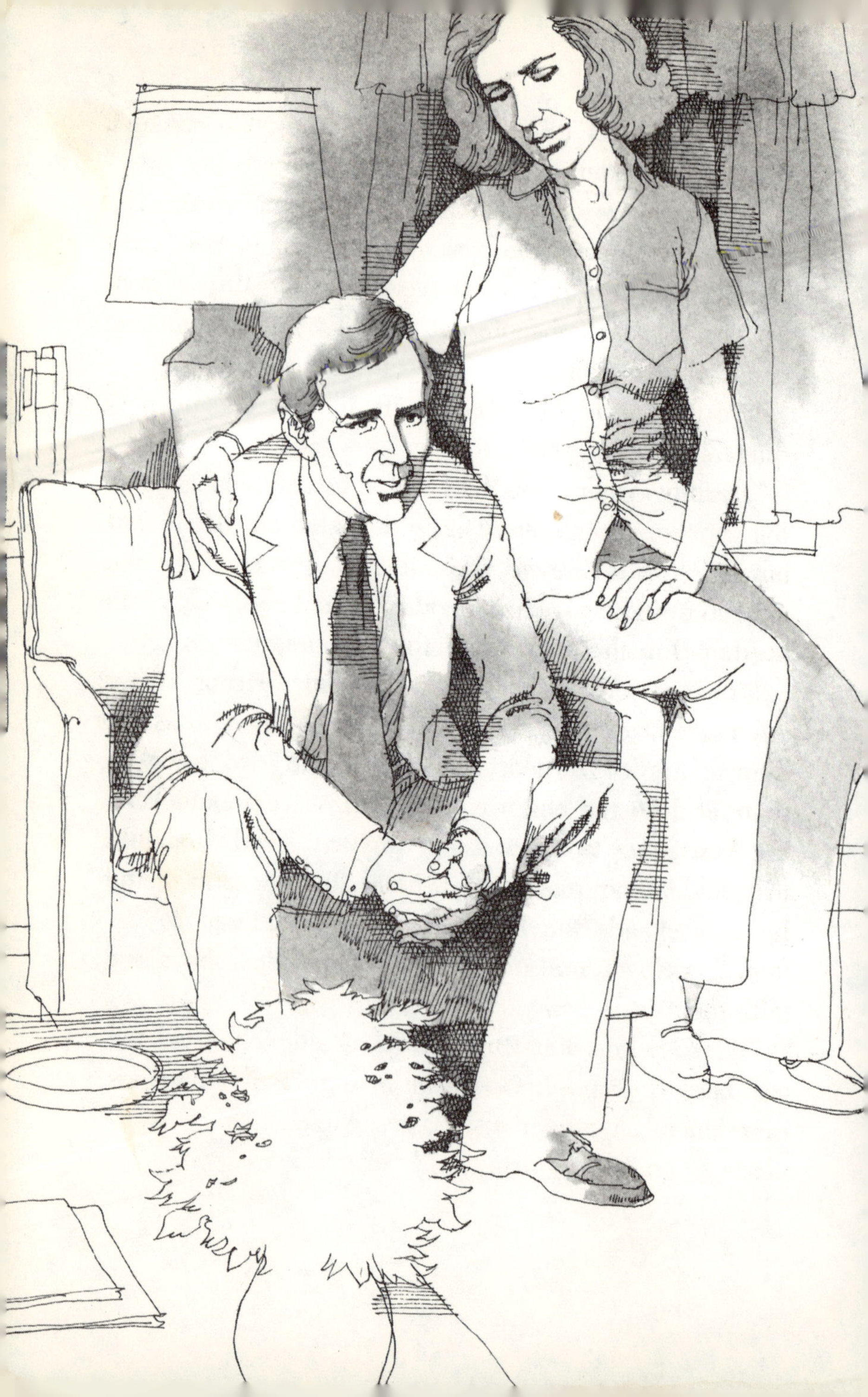

"Peter Hurley," said his wife. "There's only one time I really hate you, and that's when you're being sensible. Mr. Pestinock is wrong and you know it. The family comes first. The job comes second. You can't raise a family by putting it second all the time. There are times when the family is the most important thing and has to come first."

"Darling," said Mr. Hurley, "if I haven't got a job, the family is going to be in a real bad way."

"Keeping your job is going to split the family down the middle, and that will be a much worse way," said his wife. "Arabella and the boys need you with them. Absentee fathers aren't good for children. Children need both fathers and mothers—at home."

Mr. Hurley resolved not to tell the children about the big change for the time being, until he had had time to think it over with a clear mind. The more he thought about it, the more he became convinced that the best thing to do to keep the family together was to rent his home and find a house to rent in Phoenix for everybody. But when he broke the news to his family, they were all so glum he became impatient with them.

"Why are you all so upset?" he demanded. "We still can keep the house. Going to Arizona will be a new experience, an adventure. New people to meet, new places to go. What's wrong with that?"

"All our friends are here," said Arabella. "All the kids at school and on the beach. Gosh we were born in this town. We belong to this place."

"No beach. No surfing," said Rory. "No fishing on the pier."

"Fat lot of fishing you do on the pier," said his father. "You went once with me last summer and fell asleep."

"No baseball," said Coco.

"They play baseball all over the United States of America, Mexico, and Japan," snapped Mr. Hurley. "Also Puerto Rico and Santo Domingo and goodness knows where else."

"Dad," said Arabella very seriously. "You don't really mean that we're going to leave here, do you?"

"What else am I to do?" asked her father.

"Quit," said Arabella firmly. "Just leave them. They don't deserve you in the first place."

"And then what do we do for money?"

"Well you can get another job—somewhere around here," said Coco. "Maybe you could open a candy store," he added hopefully.

"Dad," said Arabella, "we'll make out. Gosh nobody starves in the United States. You've got lots of experience, and it wouldn't be long before you could find another job."

"Honey," said her father, "we can't get by without

money. And there's a recession on and jobs aren't that easy to get when you're over forty years of age."

"This is our home," said Arabella firmly. "And all the money in the world won't buy a home. It isn't something you buy with money. And it isn't something you sell for money. It has a value beyond money."

Mrs. Hurley looked at her daughter with surprise and admiration. "Where did you learn that?" she asked quietly.

"Oh Mother," said Arabella. "You don't learn things like that. They just are so."

"They are indeed," said Mr. Hurley. "But many people have to do a lot of suffering before they find out."

The matter wasn't decided until a couple of weeks later. By that time Mr. Hurley had listed the house for rent with a real estate agent and several prospective tenants had come by to look it over. After one of these visits Mr. Hurley found Arabella in tears in her room.

"What's the matter, honey?" he asked taking her in his arms.

"Oh, it's just wrecking everything," said Arabella. "Strangers criticizing everything in our home and going to move into it and move us out."

The next day Mr. Hurley went in to see Mr. Pestinock. "Boss," he said, "I've been thinking over that Arizona transfer. I'm going to refuse it. I've decided to stay here in California. In White's Beach."

"Hurley," said Mr. Pestinock, "that's the kind of thinking that got you into this jam in the first place. You're not putting the business first."

"That's right," said Mr. Hurley. "The business comes first sometimes. But it doesn't come first all the time. There are other values. My family and my home are one of those values."

"Your family and your home depend on your job," snapped Mr. Pestinock.

"Uh-uh," said Mr. Hurley. "My family and my home depend on me and my wife and my kids. They've nothing to do with the job." They argued some more, but Mr. Hurley was adamant that he could not move to Arizona.

"Well, if that's the way you feel about it, let me have your letter of resignation," said Mr. Pestinock at length. "You're paid monthly, so we will expect a month's notice."

Mr. Hurley shook his head. "I'm not resigning," he said. "Let's be honest about this. I'm refusing to obey instructions, so you can fire me. And since I'm paid monthly *I* expect a month's notice. Also the company owes me three weeks' vacation."

"Are you considering all the fringe benefits you're

giving up—the harvest of all your years of work?" asked Mr. Pestinock.

"The harvest of all my years of work is right in my home," said Mr. Hurley. "I'm keeping that. The rest are what you rightly call them—fringe benefits."

He went back to his office and sat down at his desk. He remembered the first time he'd sat there, promoted to an office of his own. He remembered the triumph at his home at this promotion and his wife's half-humorous inquiries about whether his secretary was young and good looking.

He remembered one little detail that had somehow seemed important to him at the time—a brand-new oversized desk blotter. He rang for his secretary, and when she came in, he said, "I'm moving out of this office. I think the new occupant will need a new desk blotter."

Then he went out and walked quickly to the elevator hoping his face didn't show how he felt.

Chapter Fourteen

By the end of June, the Yankees had cinched first place for themselves in the White's Beach Little League standings, and the Indians and Pirates were in a tie for second place. At the play-off, the Indians were ahead 5–0 at the end of three innings. Then they fell to pieces. The Pirates scored two runs on infield errors and then at the top of the fifth scored four more to put them ahead. Only one of those runs was earned. By the bottom of the sixth the Pirates had a commanding lead of 8–5, and they won handily 9–5.

It was no consolation to the Indians that six of the Pirate runs had come in on errors. Rory, who had come in to catch at the top of the sixth, was responsible for two of those errors—a wild throw to second and a passed ball with a man on third. He'd played badly and he knew it. Nor had Coco done any better. In his last game, with the lead assured, he had been put in to pitch. He walked a run home, and then another run came in on a wild pitch—and that was the end of Coco's stand on the mound.

"What's got into you?" his coach demanded of Rory at the end of the disastrous Indian game.

"I dunno," said Rory. "Just thinking of something else, I guess."

"Something else like what?" asked the coach.

"Nothing," said Rory. And that was all that could be gotten out of him. The Yankee coach fared better in questioning Coco.

"I was hoping we might put you in All Stars as a relief pitcher," he said. "But your earned run average is pretty bad. What happened the last few games?"

"My dad lost his job over the stinking Pancake Breakfast," said Coco, who was never one to hold back. "That's what happened."

The coach examined him solemnly. "That a fact?" he asked.

"Well, something like that. He was supposed to be in Hawaii, and he came back here for the Pancake Breakfast when he could have been surfing and they fired him."

"Surfing?" asked the coach.

"Sure. My dad had a good job. He used to go

surfing and golfing in Hawaii and people gave him orders for containers and stuff."

"Boy, I'd sure be upset if I lost a job like that," said the coach.

It was the job of the coaches to pick the players for All Stars, and there was never any interference with their selection. The job, of course, was to produce a balanced team, strong in all departments, and it was not easy. The best hitters all played the outfield, and to get infielders, there had to be some sacrifice in hitting strength. This produced arguments; the Oriole coach, whose team had wound up last, plunging for hitters, and the Yankee coach prepared to sacrifice hitting strength for a tight infield.

Several youngsters were shoo-ins for the All-Star team—Spider Edwards of the Yankees to head the pitchers backed by Ron Fields who had done a great job with a fast ball for the Orioles even though they had wound up in the cellar. Al Harter was a unanimous choice for catcher with Jackie Green who could also play third base as an alternate.

When the final selections had been made it was agreed that hitting strength had perhaps been whittled down a little too much in the interests of a strong defense. So they went over the roster again. Neither Rory nor Coco made that first team, but the second time around Rory's coach suggested that he should be included.

"He hits pretty good. He did well in the outfield all season, and he can fill in as a catcher."

"The last game he caught he let in two runs," said the Oriole coach.

"Nobody's infallible," said the Indian coach. "The kid's had problems. He's got guts, anyway. He made a couple of outs during the season that made up for those errors."

"We've got two catchers," said another. "What do we want with three?"

"I'm just offering you a choice between a pretty good center fielder and hitter—that's Edwards. And a pretty good center fielder, hitter, and catcher. That's Rory. My vote goes to Rory."

"You sure you're not voting that way because he was on your team and his old man ran the Pancake Breakfast?" someone asked.

"Yeah. I'm sure. He's a good kid, and now and again he looks like he could work a little magic."

"You win ball games by not making errors," said someone else. "Magic hasn't anything to do with it."

Rory's coach shook his head sadly. "Depends on your point of view," he said. "When the third baseman drops an easy fly ball it's an error on the third baseman and it's magic for the hitter. I've seen Rory block wild pitches that better catchers might have let go by. He never gives up. He's a real trier."

"So's his kid brother—Coco. But he's got the fastest wild pitch in three cities," said another.

There was some more discussion, other players' names being brought up, and at the end of the meeting the White's Beach All Stars didn't include either Rory or Coco.

"Guess we all three struck out, Dad," said Rory when he broke the news to his father.

"You think the selection was fair?" asked his father.

"Sure," said Rory. "I think I'm better than some of the guys they picked, but then I'm biased."

"Fair Schmair," said Coco. "Boy, you wait until the next Pancake Breakfast. Some of those guys are going to be in bed for a week if I have anything to do with it."

A couple of days later Larry Mack, Rory's coach, called Mr. Hurley in the evening. This was the same man that Mr. Hurley had made take down the high fence, and neither had exchanged a word with the other all season long.

"I'm sorry Rory didn't make All Stars," said Mr. Mack. "I think he should have. He had a pretty good season until the last couple of games, and then he fell off."

"I'm sorry he didn't make the team too," said Mr. Hurley. "But I'm quite sure you made the best selection you could. There'll be other years."

"None of my business," said Mr. Mack. "But I hear you lost your job over the Pancake Breakfast."

"Who told you that?" asked Mr. Hurley.

"Well, as I get it, Coco told his coach that you should have stayed surfing in Hawaii instead of coming over for the Pancake Breakfast."

"Surfing in Hawaii?" cried Mr. Hurley, and then he laughed. "It's true I lost my job," he said. "But it was a matter of moving out of White's Beach, and I didn't want to do that. Nothing to do with baseball."

"Well, I'm sorry anyway," said the coach. "You won't be going away will you, before the All-Star game?"

"Nope. Plan to stay here."

"Good. Well, I still think Rory ought to have made the team. Coco, too. See you around."

There was a week of vacation for all the players before All-Star practice started. School was now out and everybody went surfing in the early morning before the westerlies came up to spoil the shape of the waves. Rory and Coco, living close to the beach all their lives, were good surfers as was their sister, Arabella. Most of their friends kept their surfboards in the Hurley's back garden since their house was close to the beach, so they gathered there and headed for the beach together.

Ron Fields, the alternate All-Star pitcher, lived a little way from the beach and had not done as much surfing as Rory and Coco. But he was keen to improve and went out every morning whether the surf was good or not. Coco was often with him, and lent him a lighter board for Ron's was heavy and a little old-fashioned. One day they had good surf spoiled only by the fact that it had a heavy shore break. The waves held their shape almost all the way to the shore and then crested and collapsed, in very shallow water.

"Don't try too long a ride," Coco warned Ron. "Kick out in plenty of time, or you'll go over the falls and get dumped on your head."

"I'm not that good at kicking out," said Ron. "I need more practice."

"Just get out of the wave," said Coco. "That sand's real hard when you hit it."

But it seemed to Ron, watching Coco and his beach-living friends kick out expertly just before a wave crested, that this was something he ought to be able to do as well. It didn't look that hard. They just got back on the board, one foot behind the other, and swiveled the board around out of the wave. Then they dropped to their knees to paddle out and catch the next "outsider."

The more Ron studied the technique the simpler it seemed, so he tried and after several goofs began to get the hang of it.

Then came one big "outsider" with room for everybody. Rory caught it first shouting, "Gangway, you mudhens." Then Coco caught it and Pete Reilly (who didn't play baseball) and Tony Melotti and Randy Day, who was the All-Star left fielder. Ron was the last to catch it and on this vast hill of a wave in came six glittering boys on six gleaming boards arrowing for the beach.

Coco was the first to realize that this was no ordinary "outsider." There was what seemed to be a wall of water behind him and a valley of water in front of him. He glanced to the side and behind him, shifted his weight back on the board and slewed it around. The board rose over the top of the wave and dropped down the other side. Peter Reilly and Tony Melotti dropped out an instant later. Tony, seeing a little ahead of him a dry beach and little else, just dived off his board into the wall of the wave and held his breath until it had gone by.

Those two were the last to make it. The next second the wave crested and exploded. It collapsed with a noise like gunfire. There was scarcely a foot of water beneath it when the wave exploded, and the remaining surfers were flung into the shallow water with enormous force. Coco saw Rory's blue board flip up into the air like a pip squeezed out of an orange. Another board—Randy's—turned end over end before coming down sideways in the turmoil. Then the surf seethed angrily up the beach and in the "soup" Coco saw the three other surfers, one crouched in the water and the other two staggering up toward the beach.

The one crouching down got up slowly and crawled up the beach too and Coco recognized his friend Ron. He paddled in to see that everything was all right. Ron was bleeding a little from the nose and rubbing his left leg.

"What happened?" asked Coco.

"I tried to kick out, and that board came round and hit me like a door," said Ron. "The wave just took it and flung it at me."

"Your nose is bleeding," said Coco.

"That's not what hurts. It's my leg. Boy, I caught it right on the knee. It hurts right up to my ears."

"See if you can walk," said Coco.

"You crazy?"

"Well, just put a little weight on it."

Ron, wiping the blood from his nose with his arm, tried and groaned. "Give it a little time," he said. "Man that thing hurts." In a while, the pain got less, but that was the end of surfing that day for Ron. The only other surfer hurt was Randy Day. His right

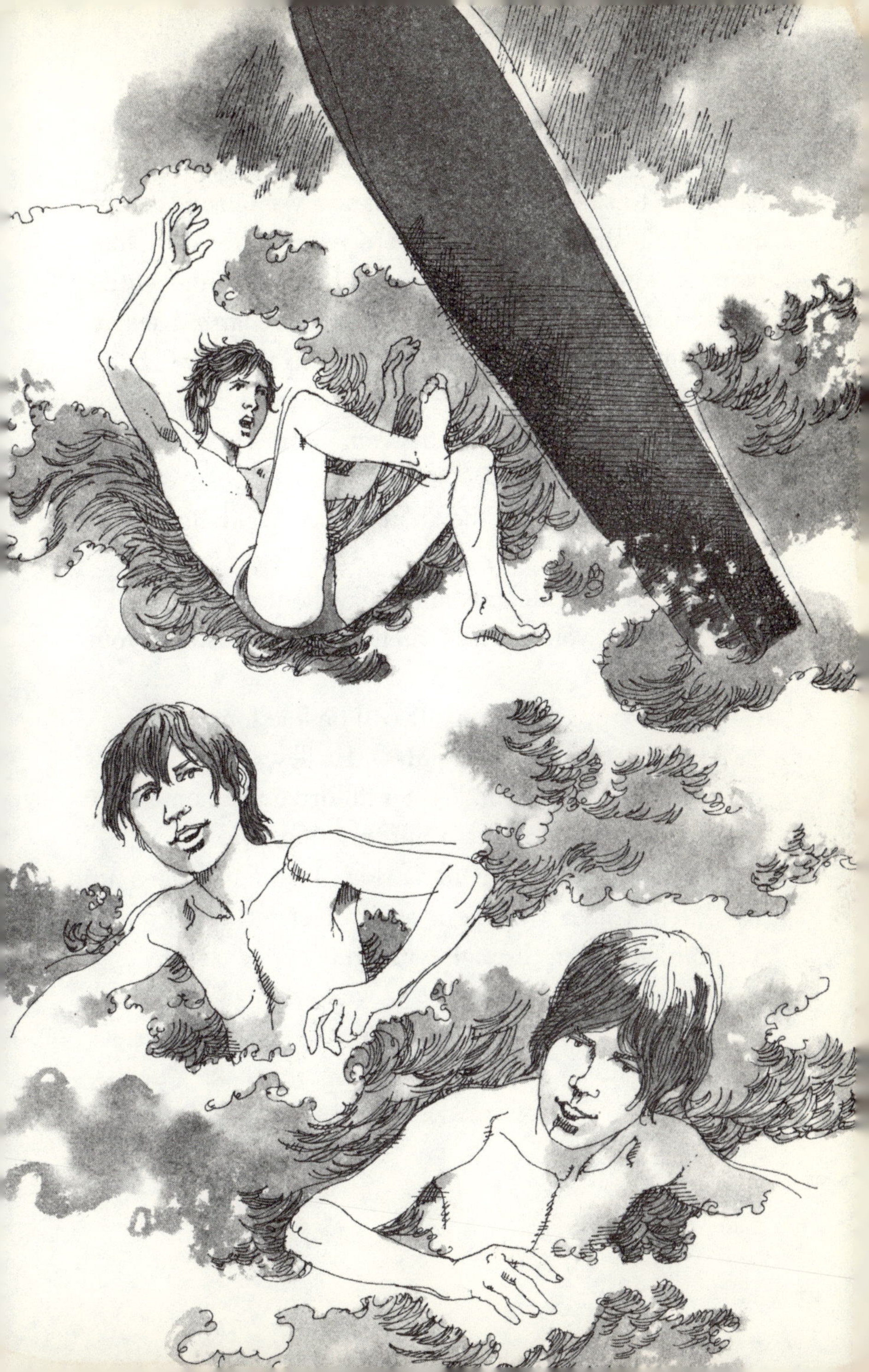

thumb was swollen and he had lost a little skin seemingly from coming down on the sand and putting his hand out to save himself. But Randy was an old surfer and didn't think his hurts were enough to stop him going in again. In he went and they surfed for a little while more, and then all brought their boards back to Rory's house where Mrs. Hurley fixed them hamburgers.

"What's the matter with you, Ron?" asked Mrs. Hurley noticing his limp.

"I got wiped out in the shore break," said Ron. "But it's all right."

Mrs. Hurley watched him walk about and said, "I'd better drive you home when you've finished your hamburger."

"It's nothing," said Ron. "It will be fine tomorrow."

"Maybe it will," said Mrs. Hurley. "But today's today, and it isn't fine today. So I'll drive you home."

"Me too," said Randy. "I hurt my thumb."

"Okay, I'll give you all a ride. Just don't mess up my kitchen floor with your sandy feet, or you'll *all* be limping when I'm through with you."

Chapter Fifteen

The White's Beach All Stars dreamed, like every other Little League All Stars in the country, of getting to Williamsport for the Little League World Series. But everybody knew it was only a dream and they rarely survived more than one or two games of the local play-offs.

There were many reasons for this. One was that there were only a limited number of boys from whom to choose All-Star players—a total of four teams. Other cities had six or eight teams and so a wider choice. Again, during the season, playing only against the same four teams, they did not get as much experience as other All-Star teams. Lastly, being close to the beach, baseball wasn't the main attraction for the boys of the town. There was surfing and sailing as well, and added to that scuba diving and fishing. So not everybody "went out" for baseball.

Still, this year it was generally agreed that the All-Star team was above standard, and with luck they might get to the semifinals. Their traditional rival—the team that always eliminated them—was El Redondo, which had twice got to within a game of representing Western America, only to be eliminated by a team from Reno, Nevada, one year, and Seattle, Washington, the next.

So for the White's Beach All Stars, the cry was not "Williamsport or Bust" but "Beat El Redondo." It was a brave cry but so far had proved hopeless.

Although they were not on the All-Star team, Rory and Coco turned up to help with practice. All the boys on the team were their friends, and Coco could pitch batting practice and Rory catch. Larry Mack was the All-Star coach and Joe Sevri his assistant. As soon as Larry Mack saw Rory he called him over.

"You're in luck," he said. "Podranski's dad is taking his vacation early and going down fishing off Mexico. He's taking Chuck with him. So you get to play center field."

"As an alternate?" asked Rory.

"No. You'll start at center field. If we go beyond the first game, I might need you to catch. That dumb kid Randy Day has got a swollen thumb."

Rory said nothing.

"He hurt it surfing," said Mack.

"I know," said Rory. "He went over the falls. But I think he's going to be able to catch. Randy's pretty tough."

"We'll see," said Mack.

Joe Sevri, the assistant coach, who had been coaching the Orioles all the season, decided to make it his job to "beef up" the hitters, as he put it. White's Beach had a pitching machine, but Joe Sevri didn't like pitching machines. They were all right for sharpening up a batter's timing, but in his view a batter needed to watch a pitcher's windup. He had found that even poor hitters, after a while, could hit the pitching machine. Joe's idea was to have as many different pitchers as possible throw batting practice. "Swing at what you think you can hit," he told the batters. "Strike zone or not, if you can hit it, swing. I want you to be aggressive—not waiting for a walk."

All the All-Star pitchers were called on to pitch batting practice and the coach noticed that Ron Fields was throwing only slow balls. "Steam it in there, Ron," he said. "Mix it up. I don't want them to see that ball. Just hear it hiss as it goes by."

"Coach," said Ron. "I hurt my knee the other day and I don't want to come down too hard on it for a while."

"Hurt it doing what?"

"Surfing."

"Surfing?" cried Joe. "If they'd just move the beach a hundred miles from this city, we might have a chance of getting to Williamsport. You know Randy Day hurt his hand surfing?"

"Yes," said Ron. "Same wave."

"Swell," said Joe sarcastically. "Okay. Take it easy. But let me have a look at that knee after practice. You been to the doctor?"

"No. It's just a bruise."

The coach looked about and saw Coco behind the net. "Hey, Coco," he said, "see if you can steam a few in. Don't hit anyone though."

"You want me to try and strike him out or you want me to give him something he can hit?" asked Coco.

"I want you to throw your best pitches and see if he can hit them," said the coach.

So Coco threw a fast ball and got hit to the outfield, and a slow ball and got hit, and a change-up and got hit. Then he threw his Krazy Kevin pitch and the batter swung at it so hard that he fell down. He also missed.

"Hey," said the coach who had been standing behind the mound, "what kind of a pitch was that?"

"Krazy Kevin pitch," said Coco.

"Can you throw it any time you want?"

"Uh-uh. I can throw it most times. Maybe about

eighty percent of the time. Only thing is, nobody can catch it—only my brother."

"Throw it again," said the coach.

Coco threw it again and again the batter missed.

"That fool thing goes up when it crosses the plate," said the coach. "Throw another." This one was so wild that the batter didn't even bother to swing. But the next one was a beauty. It seemed to dance its way around the bat. The batter swung again, and missed again.

"How come you didn't show us this pitch during the season?" asked the coach.

"I was working on it," said Coco. "But it wasn't very reliable and my brother Kevin told me to forget it."

The coach signaled to Ken Ishiwara who was lead-off man for the All Stars as he had been for the Indians. Ken was small and compact and wore glasses with rims so big they looked like lamps in front of his face. But all season long he had struck out only four times, getting on base either with a walk or a little rap through the infield. He ran so fast that he could sometimes beat out a throw from third base if the third baseman made even the slightest fumble. He had the record for stolen bases in the League.

"See what you can do against Ken," said the coach to Coco.

"You want the Krazy Kevin pitch?" asked Coco.

"He's your problem," said the coach. "See if you can strike him out."

Coco knew that Ken had an eagle eye, and since he was short in stature didn't like a letter-high ball on the outside corner. "Can Rory catch me?" he asked.

The coach shrugged and signaled to Rory, who came over and squatted down behind the plate, but gave no signal. Coco tried with the letter-high ball, fast, and missed. He tried again and missed, and Rory signaled for low and inside. But Coco shook off the sign and tried a fast ball inside and a little high. It popped up, out of play. He threw another letter-high fast ball, and over the outside corner, and this time his control was perfect and Ken let it go by. Ken's favorite ball, Coco knew, was a fast ball right down the middle. Rory called for every ball but that, and Coco shook off all the signals.

Then he wound up and put everything he had into the fast ball. Ken just wasn't looking for his favorite pitch. The ball took him by surprise. He swung late and struck out. Coco went on pitching, and Ken asked him to throw one of the Krazy Kevin pitches. He threw it and Ken laid down a perfect bunt.

"You hit it," said Coco surprised.

"Sure. You can hit anything if you know what is coming," said Ken.

Meanwhile, the two coaches had been conferring.

When they finished Joe Sevri came over to Coco. "We left one alternate spot open on All Stars," he said. "You know what that means? The guy chosen doesn't get to play unless somebody's injured. Right?"

"Right."

"Okay. You're going to be the alternate. Work on that crazy pitch of yours. We may need it to beat El Redondo."

"El Redondo?" said Coco. "Who are they? Williamsport, here we come." He wound up and threw and the ball was so wild it missed the backstop.

Sevri walked off shaking his head.

Chapter Sixteen

Mr. Hurley, following his wife's advice, didn't start looking around for employment immediately after leaving the Safehold Corporation. He wanted to, but his wife insisted that after fourteen years of solid work, with only three-week vacations each year, he should take at least a couple of months off.

"That's going to dig a hole in our savings," he said.

"Not much of a hole," said Mrs. Hurley. "And you need a rest."

"How can I rest when I'm out of work?" asked Mr. Hurley.

"That proves it," said his wife. "If you have to have a job to feel secure, you're sick. So better do without the job for a while, until you can feel secure without one." Although Mr. Hurley didn't quite agree with this piece of reasoning, he decided that he would wait for a while until the news that he was no longer with Safehold got around and see what offers came his way. Probably none—not because of his worth but because of the depressed state of business—and his age. Meanwhile he had an opportunity to do a number of things around the house and get a glimpse of the world and his neighbors without thinking of container sales.

One of the things he liked to do was go fishing off the pier. There were bonita and mackerel to be caught and occasionally a halibut. He had once caught an eight-pound halibut off the pier, and the memory of that catch had sustained him through hours of waiting for a bite. Down on the pier he met Al Flint, who was surprised to see him.

"What are you doing here?" asked Al.

"What are you doing here?" asked Mr. Hurley.

"Fishing—and fighting an ulcer," said Al. "As of this moment, the fish and the ulcer are winning."

"Tell me about it," said Mr. Hurley.

"Oh, it's nothing new," said Al. "In my line by the time you get the building permit you can't get the cement. When you've got the cement lined up and poured, the carpenters are on strike. Carpenters come back to work and the banks start raising their prime rate . . . Just good old-fashioned hassling that nobody ever taught me about at school. What's your trouble?"

"I quit," said Mr. Hurley and explained the situation.

"Well, what do you know," said Al Flint when Mr. Hurley had finished. "You mean you gave up a good job just to stay in the old neighborhood?"

"Well," said Mr. Hurley lamely, "it was Arabella and the boys. They wouldn't be happy anywhere else. What's the good of a job if your kids are miserable. But I don't want to blame them. I made the decision. I'll probably find something."

"Sure," said Al Flint, with perhaps a touch too much heartiness. Then he added, "Your bait's dead. You need to freshen it or you'll catch nothing." Whether this comment referred obliquely to his job hunting, Mr. Hurley could not decide, but he reeled his line in and put a fresh bait on his hook.

On his way home from the pier, Al Flint stopped in at Heinz's bakery to pick up some rolls and a pie for dinner. Heinz, who had been at work since three in the morning, was still there.

"Trouble with the brickwork in one of the ovens," he said by way of explanation. "Should be relined, but I hate to do it. Do anything to an oven and all the temperatures are wrong." He put a large Danish pastry into a sack. "Take that home to the missus," he said. "No charge. She likes them."

"Thanks," said Al. "No offense, but you know how much she's put on diet plans so far this year—doctors and all? Two hundred dollars. Thirty-cent pastry and she'll blow it all."

"Al," said Mr. Heinz, "you gotta keep up with the times. Women's lib. You know. They got as much right to be happy and weak as men. Give her the pastry."

"Okay," said Al. "You heard about Pete Hurley losing his job?"

"Pete Hurley? No."

Al explained.

"Guy like that is a valuable man," said Mr. Heinz. "Someone ought to snap him up."

"He's the wrong side of forty," said Al.

"So's the whole of the Supreme Court and most of the Congress," said Mr. Heinz. "If I hear of anything, I'll let him know."

"Yeah—you might spread the word around," said Al. "You want the oven relined with fire brick, I'll do it for you. Just the cost of materials and handling."

Mr. Heinz considered this in some surprise. Al Flint was known as an excellent builder. But he never worked for nothing.

"How come?" Mr. Heinz demanded. "You don't owe me anything."

"I don't know 'how come,'" said Al Flint. "Something to do with Hurley. Money. Jobs. They're not everything."

"Try to get by without them," said Mr. Heinz.

Before he went home, however, Mr. Heinz put a notice in his shop window. It read, "Under 10 and over 60, donuts half price. Fridays only."

"Why did you do that?" asked his wife when he told her of it.

"I don't know why I did it," said Mr. Heinz. "Something to do with Pete Hurley."

To everyone's surprise White's Beach won its first All-Star game. Lots were drawn to establish which teams would play for the district championship, and by good luck White's Beach drew Westham as its first opponent.

Westham was a small town, not much bigger than White's Beach, so the odds were about even, and White's Beach won 6–4.

Ken Ishiwara, at first base, was the hero of the game, hitting a triple at the top of the seventh with a man on second and a man on third to drive in the two winning runs.

The surprising thing was that Ken was not a long-ball hitter. But the pitcher had made the mistake of challenging him with a fast ball right down the middle, and it dropped between center and left field.

With Westham eliminated in the first game, White's Beach now faced Toddstown West, who had won their first round of the eliminations. Toddstown was a much bigger city than White's Beach, with far more ballplayers. They had two All-Star teams—the East team and the West team. The East team had gone down to El Redondo, White's Beach greatest rival. They had gone down 8–1, and the rumor went around that El Redondo was blazing hot that year.

"Never mind El Redondo," said Larry Mack, the chief coach. "We've got to get Toddstown West first. If we don't beat them, we're out of it. So let's concentrate on that job."

"Aren't we allowed one loss?" asked Ken Ishiwara, the team captain.

"No," said Mack. "One loss and we're out of competition. So let's make this the year that we beat El Redondo."

Spider Edwards had pitched four full innings of the first game. Against Toddstown West, Ron Fields opened up for White's Beach. There was no score until the third inning and then, when the Toddstown lead-off man came to bat, Ron began to lose his stuff. He walked the lead man, and the second man up was hit by the ball and got on base. This called for a meeting at the mound and Mack asked Ron how he felt.

"Okay," said Ron. "I just lost my rhythm for a while."

"How's that leg?" asked the coach. "Holding up?"

153

"It's okay so far," said Ron.

"What do you think?" asked the coach turning to Randy Day, who was catching. Randy shrugged. "Just two bad pitches. This is only the third. I think he can make it."

"I'm going to leave you in," said Mack. "Remember you got seven guys out there ready to make outs. Don't kill yourself."

The next batter was out on a pop fly behind the plate, but Ron walked the fourth man, loading the bases with only one out. The coach faced a difficult decision. He could hold Spider in reserve in case of extra innings and put in Jackie Green, who was playing third base, and fill the third-base spot from the dugout. Or he could put in Spider who, however, could only pitch three innings under the rules and would have to come out. He couldn't use Coco unless a player was hurt in the game—the injury Ron was suffering from he had brought into the game with him. He decided to stick with Ron for a while, and Ron came through for him. The runner on third scored on a long fly ball to center field caught by Rory, which made two outs. But the third out Ron made easily on a comebacker with a throw to first, which retired the side.

White's Beach failed to tie the score at the top of the fourth. Stammers got on with a rap right over second base between the shortstop and second baseman, but Dusty Martin, who followed him, hit into a double play. The next batter flied out to left field.

Everybody went out on the field worrying about the pitcher, and there was need to worry. Ron walked the first two batters, though some of the calls were dubious. He was taken out of the game and Jackie Green sent to the mound in relief. Jackie had pitched in relief through the season, though mostly he played third base. He had a good eye and a strong arm, but he hadn't got a really fast ball. Still, he struck out the next batter and then came a short rap to the second baseman which could have been a double play. But though the out was made at second, the ball didn't get to first base in time, leaving runners on third and first. The next batter hit a shot right back to the mound. Jackie was off balance. He couldn't get the ball and he couldn't get out of the way, and was hit, and went down as if he had been clubbed. The runner on third scored, and Jackie sat on the ground groaning and rubbing his ankle.

"Let's have a look at that," said Coach Mack, who was the first to get to him. They took off his shoe and sock, and the flesh over the ankle bone showed the pattern of the sock imprinted on it by the blow. It was already swelling and turning blue. Jackie had to be helped back to the dugout and Spider Edwards

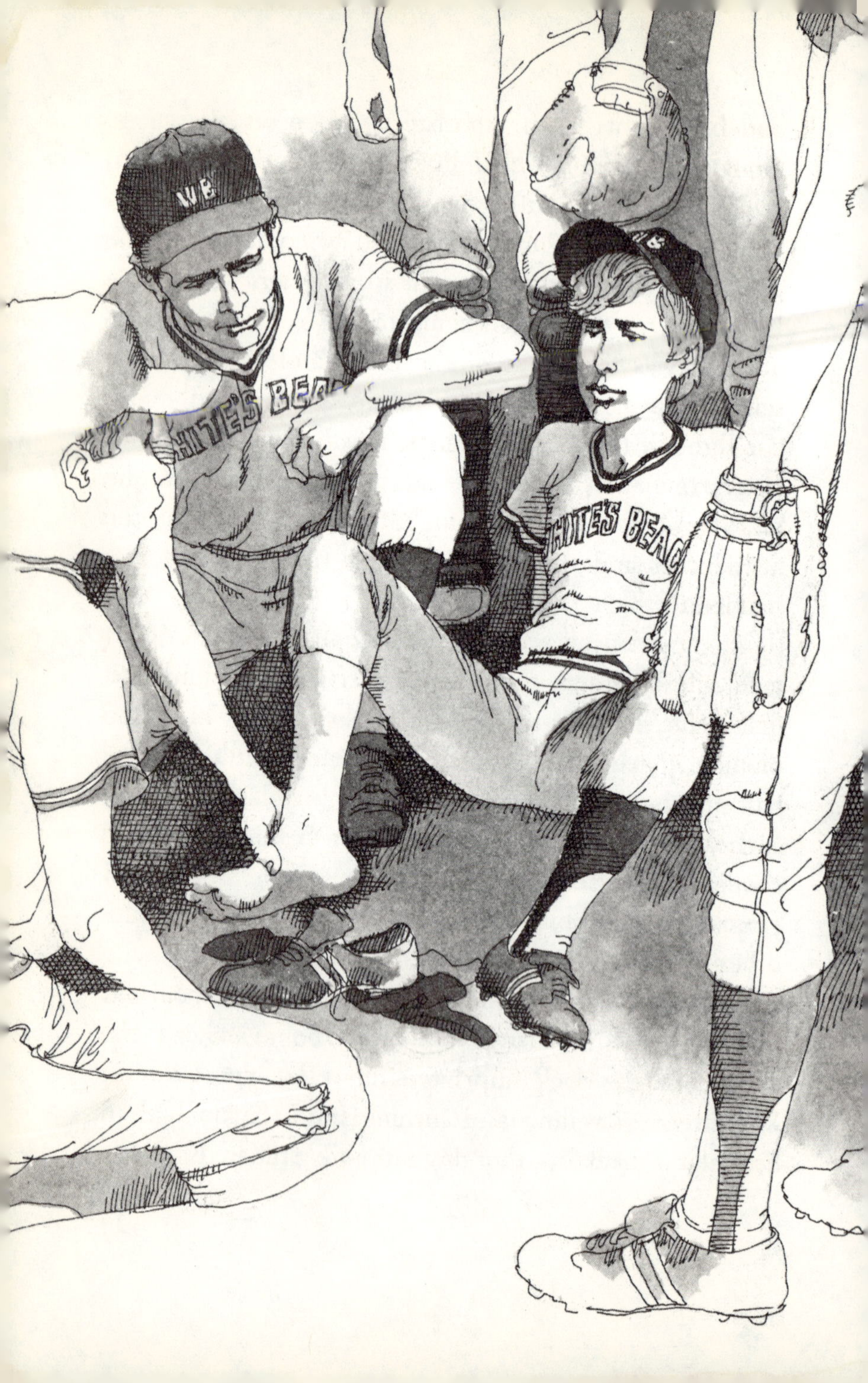
WB
HITE'S BEA
HITE'S BEAC

came in to pitch, with two and a third innings to go, a man on second and a man on third. However, he struck out the third batter without trouble and the score was Toddstown West, 2, and White's Beach, 0.

Things went better for White's Beach after that. They scored two runs in the fifth to tie the score. Then Rory came up to bat in the top of the sixth and with a runner at second and two outs, he hit the ball through the center to bring the run in, putting White's Beach one run ahead. The next man up popped out, and Toddstown came up to bat with one run needed to tie the score and go into extra innings, and two needed to win.

The first batter was walked, but the second hit into a double play and, with one out left in the game, Spider went into his windup and threw a little high and outside. The batter swung, connected, and the ball soared up and away toward left field. Higher and higher it went, with the left fielder fading back, and the home run cleared the fence, tying the score. Spider struck out the next batter, giving White's Beach another turn at bat in extra innings.

Toddstown West had put in a relief pitcher in the fourth and now changed the pitcher again for the extra innings. He pitched well, but he was unlucky. With two outs and a man on third, an outfielder dropped a fly ball and a run scored. At the end of the inning, with Toddstown West still to bat, White's Beach was one run ahead.

Technically, Spider could now pitch two-thirds of an inning but no more. Coach Mack explained the situation to the umpires so that everything could be understood. "I have one pitcher injured in the game," he said, "and I'm entitled to use my alternate pitcher."

"Who's your alternate pitcher?" asked the home-plate umpire.

"Coco Hurley. He'll be wearing a Yankee uniform—gray with blue letters, because as an alternate he didn't get an All-Star uniform."

"Okay," said the home-plate umpire. He turned to the Toddstown coach who had come over to see what was going on. "Okay with you?" he asked.

"Yeah, that's okay with me," said the coach grinning.

Spider made the first out with one pitch which was popped up to the catcher. He walked the next batter who promptly stole second. The next hit a blooper over the shortstop's head putting a man on first and a man on third and one out. The next batter flied out to third and that made two outs and Spider had to come out of the game.

"Go get him, Coco," said the coach giving him the ball. "Two outs. That's the tying run on third and the winning run on first. No wild pitches."

"Coach," said Coco. "Could Rory catch me? We've been working together all year, and he knows how to catch that Krazy Kevin pitch—if I can throw it."

"Okay," said the coach.

So Randy went out to center field and Rory came in to catch and Coco's first five warm-up pitches were so wild that the Toddstown dugout was on its feet jeering at him. The sixth was in the dirt, and after Rory had blocked it he walked the ball back out to the mound.

"Steady down, Coco," he said. "Take it easy. Take a few deep breaths. You feeling okay?"

"Sure I'm feeling okay," said Coco. "Just one lousy pitch, and I've thrown away the ball game. Why shouldn't I feel okay?"

"The hitter's feeling just as bad as you," said Rory. "He's the last out. Keep the ball down, that's all."

Coco's first pitch was low and in the dirt, but Rory blocked it. So was the second. The third pitch was so high that Rory only got it by jumping up, and again he walked the ball back to the mound. The Toddstown dugout was going wild yelling. Rory gave the ball to Coco and said, "One more pitch like that and I'm gonna come out here and bust you one on the nose. Take your time."

Back at the plate Rory signaled for a curve ball and the signal was shaken off. He signaled for a change-up and that was shaken off. He signaled for a fast ball, and Coco nodded. It was a beauty; knee high and on the outside corner for strike one. The hitter looked at the batting coach and got the sign to take, for the coach was banking on Coco's reputation for wild pitching. It was a mistake. The next ball was a fast ball too and in the same place, and the batter just stood looking at it.

"The count was now three and two. Coco now tried a change-up, but the batter was expecting it and fouled it off. He fouled off the next two pitches, and Coco stepped off the rubber and took a look around. Randy at center field seemed to be playing too much to his right and Coco waved him over. He looked at the left fielder and the right fielder, and he did all this to persuade the hitter that the next ball was likely to be a fast ball which would go a long way if he connected. The hitter looked at his coach and got his signal to swing, and Coco shook off every signal Rory gave him.

"That kid's my brother," said Rory to the batter. "He's a real idiot. He wants to throw a fast ball." The batter called for time and stepped out of the box. Rory got up off his haunches and stole a look at the home-plate umpire. He fancied he could detect a smile on his face.

The batter stepped back into the box again and the

umpire signaled Coco to play ball. Coco stepped on the rubber, went into his windup, and threw. It wasn't a fast ball or a change-up or a slider.

It was the Krazy Kevin pitch. The batter started to swing and then held up. The ball looked as if it was going to be low and outside. But at the last moment it swooped up and at the same time flicked inward and crossed the plate right over the strike zone. For a moment the umpire stared and then, holding up his right fist, shouted, "Strike three! You're out."

The whole team exploded out of the dugout to Coco, thumping him and roughing up his hair. White's Beach had miraculously won two games. Something they hadn't done in years. One more game and they would be district champions—for the first time in their history.

But that one game would be against their great rivals—El Redondo.

Chapter Seventeen

The district that included White's Beach had ten All-Star teams. The first play-offs, which White's Beach survived by beating Westham, left five teams. The next play-off, which White's Beach again won by beating Toddstown West, left three teams still in competition—one of the five having drawn a bye. Lots were now drawn to determine which of these three remaining teams would face each other for the next round, and White's Beach was lucky and drew the bye. That meant that White's Beach would meet the victor of the encounter between the two remaining teams—their old rivals, El Redondo, and Warren, the other team which had survived so far.

El Redondo was confident of winning and then, by beating White's Beach two days later, wrapping up the district championship. There was solid reason for their confidence. In their two games so far they had won 8–1 and 7–0. Their pitching was tremendous and so was their hitting. But as Coach Mack kept pointing out to his players, the great thing about El Redondo was that they didn't make any mistakes and took advantage of every opportunity offered. They never missed a double play, and the single run which had been scored against them so far was a home run.

"And a home run's a fluke," said Mack. "Nobody in the world, and that includes Babe Ruth, could ever be sure of hitting a home run."

"Babe Ruth pointed to the place in the stands where he was going to hit a ball once," said Rory, who had just read a book about him.

"And nobody in that whole ball park was more surprised than Babe Ruth when it happened," replied Mack. "In the infield or the outfield expect the ball to come to you—every time. Be literally on your toes—heels off the ground, crouched down and body leaning forward when the pitcher goes into his windup. Figure in advance of the play what you are going to do with the ball when you get it. Remember the prime rule is to throw to the base ahead of the runner. Don't be caught surprised, with the ball in your hand."

Having drawn the bye, the White's Beach team went to see the game between Warren and El Redondo. Warren was a small inland community whose high school did well in sports, though better at football than basketball. Their best pitcher couldn't be used because he had already pitched the allowable number of innings that week. The other starting pitcher had a fair fast ball and a really great change-up, which slumped down unexpectedly over the plate through the strike zone. He struck out three in the first two innings, mostly on the change-up. Then a man got aboard on a sharp rap past the third baseman. The pitcher, facing a new batter, made the mistake of trying the fast ball on him. The hitter connected with a triple and the run came home.

Thereafter El Redondo dominated the play. They were also compelled to use their second-string pitcher. He had a wicked fast ball, even though it tended to be wild, and a slider. So the pitchers were about even. But Warren made a couple of infield errors which cost them, and the El Redondo batting strength was easily superior. El Redondo won 7–4 though Warren, battling gamely, had bases loaded at the final out.

That game took place on a Saturday. There was no game scheduled for Sunday, so the encounter between El Redondo and White's Beach for the district championship took place on the following Monday afternoon.

On Monday Mr. Hurley, who had been job hunting

since his talk on the pier with Al Flint, had an appointment in downtown Los Angeles with a Mr. Truxton of Western Pipe and Appliance Corporation who had advertised for experienced sales personnel. The company's offices were in Denver, Colorado, but the appointment was to be held in a suite of rooms in the Biltmore Hotel in Pershing Square. Mr. Hurley had been in the Biltmore Hotel many times, but never with such feelings of anxiety and inadequacy. As soon as he was out of range of the cooling effect of the ocean, and the combination of dazzling sun and hot concrete, which marked the approach of Los Angeles, smote him, he began to feel uneasy. The uneasiness increased the nearer he got to Pershing Square and by the time he had parked his car he felt depressed and nervous.

There were a number of other applicants, most of them younger than he, ahead of Mr. Hurley. It was an hour before his turn for an interview came, but Mr. Truxton, dressed out of style in a crew cut and rimless glasses and suit of light gray flannel, was easygoing and had soon put Mr. Hurley at his ease.

Still the interview did not go well. The crucial question was whether Mr. Hurley would be prepared to move from territory to territory as the company required. To this he plainly had to reply, no.

"That's a pity," said Mr. Truxton. "You might give

it some thought. Your credentials and experience are just what we need, but our salesmen have to be willing to move around. It's our experience that when they get settled in a particular territory, they begin to overlook opportunities for new sales. That's one of the reasons," he added, "why we prefer younger men."

"I know the California and Hawaii area well," said Mr. Hurley. "I've good connections. But we are settled. Children in school, our own house, and so on. It was over the question of moving that I left my last employment." Mr. Truxton nodded. He looked like he might be in his fifties himself.

"I understand," he said. "Believe me, I know that as time goes by moving isn't easy. Well, we'll be in touch." His handshake was friendly, but Mr. Hurley knew he hadn't got the job and, if he held to his view, there were a lot more jobs he wasn't going to get.

"Don't worry," said his wife, when he reported to her. "There's some company that wants you very badly. It's just a matter of making contact."

"I guess so," said Mr. Hurley. Then he brightened. "I ought to get down to the ball game," he said. "Those kids will need a cheering section. However," he added, "they haven't washed the dog in weeks."

"Consistency," said Mrs. Hurley. "It's one of their strong points."

Everybody on the ball team had reported to Valley

Park in El Redondo an hour before game time, and it seemed to Rory and Coco and everybody else on the White's Beach team that the El Redondo players had all grown about a foot since the last time they saw them.

"I shouldn't have eaten that piece of chocolate cake," said Coco.

"You didn't eat a piece of chocolate cake," said Rory.

"I did too. Last Friday," said Coco. "It's still fighting it out down there."

Even during the warm-up, with El Redondo watching, the whole team was tense and ill at ease and misfielded balls. Spider Edwards was to pitch with Ron Fields to back him up. Al Harter would be catching and Rory playing center field, and since White's Beach were the visitors, they batted first.

"Listen," said Coach Mack, gathering the team around him for a last word. "Don't think of what they're going to do to you. Think of what you're going to do to them. Be aggressive. Get out there and hit. They've had their wins. Now its time for their losses."

Ken Ishiwara led off and got on base with a line drive that went between the first and second basemen. Stammers, the shortstop, popped out to the catcher, and Tony Melotti, at second base, struck out. Then Ken, overanxious and with two outs, tried to steal second and was caught, and that ended the first inning. Still, once the game had started some of the nervousness went and the first two innings were barren—neither side gaining a run, which increased the confidence of White's Beach.

Rory lead off the top of the third to be followed by Al Harter, who was catching, and then Spider Edwards, who, like most pitchers, was not much good at bat.

Rory was feeling tense when he came to the plate. Playing center field, he had had no part of the action so far, and he knew that only action would relieve his nervousness. He looked at Joe Sevri, who was coaching at third, and Joe gave him the signal to take. He took, and the pitch was called a strike. Joe signaled him to take again, and that was a ball as was the pitch that followed on which he did not swing. The count was two and one, and Joe signaled for him to take on the next pitch. The next pitch was a ball also, but it was a little high and outside and that was where Rory like them. Ignoring the coach's signal he swung anyway. He connected solidly and the ball streaked over the first baseman to drop before the right fielder could get to it.

Rory was aboard with a single and Al Harter came to the plate. Al was not a good hitter. In fact, during the season he developed a habit of hitting into double

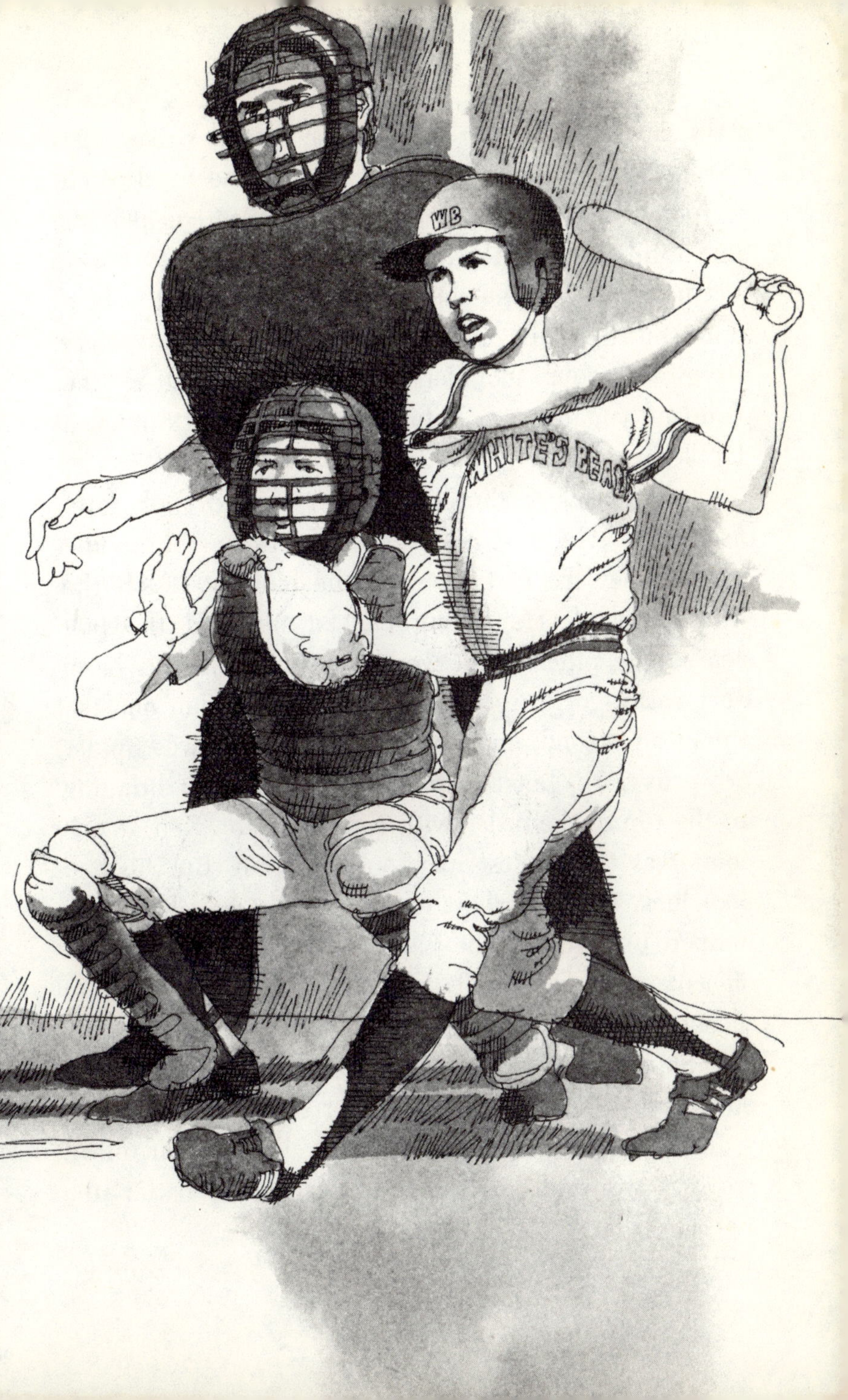
WB
WHITE'S BEAC

plays. He took on the first, which was a strike, and took on the second, which was a ball. The third pitch he fouled over the backstop, and Joe Sevri called for time and beckoned Al over to him.

"Choke up, Al," he said. "And move up in the box. Your stance is just a little too open. Get your head down and your shoulders and hips parallel to the plate, or you're a cinch to hit to the shortstop for a double play."

Al went back to the box, moved up and choked up on the bat. The next pitch was right down the middle and he knew he had to swing the moment it left the pitcher's hand. He swung choked up, and the ball cleared the pitcher and went clean over second base. Rory easily got to second, so there was a man on first, a man on second, and nobody out. Now it was Spider Edwards' turn, but he was quickly struck out bringing up the top of the order with Ken Ishiwara. Ken at this point was the coolest man on the team. But he had poor luck. He hit a short rap to the first baseman, who jumped up and got the ball. Al Harter, on first, took off as soon as he heard the ball hit and got safely to second, while Rory, on second, had moved to third. But Stammers was out on a long fly ball, and that ended the White's Beach threat for that inning.

In the bottom of the third El Redondo went ahead scoring two runs. Spider walked the first batter—the first walk of the game—got the second, but hit the third, who then took his base.

The next man hit a long shot to right field which just missed clearing the fence, bringing the two men on base home. The batter got to second and the next man was walked. But then came a brilliant double play—a ground ball to the third baseman for the force and then a long throw to first to get the runner, and that ended the inning.

At the top of the fourth El Redondo made a pitching change, to everyone's surprise, for their pitcher had been doing well. It was a mistake, for Melotti, coming up for White's Beach promptly hit the first pitch to right field for a double, and Green moved him over to third, getting to first safely. The next two flied out, and Rory, coming up to the plate, represented the tying run.

"Hit whatever you can," said Mack as he left the dugout. "Don't be careless, but be aggressive."

Rory swung at the first two pitches and missed. Joe Sevri called him over.

"You're the third out," he said. "Never mind the long fly ball. Choke up good. Nice little rap through the hole at second base is as good as a home run right now." So Rory choked up and took the next two pitches which were low, leaving the count two and two. The pitcher missed with the next ball as well, and Rory glanced at the third-base coach, who gave him the signal to swing.

With the count at three and two, the pitcher knew he had to throw a strike, and he did, waist high and on the outside corner. He steamed the ball in there and Rory met it with the bat choked. He swung harder than he thought and a little late, for the ball soared upward and away, midway between center and right field. The center fielder and the right fielder both converged on the ball, calling, and right fielder lunged for it. He got the ball in his glove, rolled over, and came up with the glove empty. Two runs scored and Rory got to second. Now it was the catcher's spot —Al Harter.

Joe Sevri weighed the possibilities. "I'm going to gamble," he said to Al. "Swing away until they've got two strikes on you, if that's what happens. But on that third strike, when they're expecting you to swing again, I want you to try to lay down a bunt. Yes. A bunt. I know you're the third out, but if you lay it down good, they won't be expecting it, and we just might get away with it."

"You want me to bunt with two strikes on me?" asked Al, surprised.

"Right. I'm going to give you the sign to swing, in case they know our signs, but I want you to bunt."

Al could expect the pitcher to concentrate on

strikes, and he was right. The first two were beauties —a change-up and a slider, both of which found the strike zone and both of which Al swung on and missed. As the pitcher released the next pitch Al squared around. Too late the infield realized that he was going to bunt. The pitch was a fast ball down the middle and a little low. Al got his bat on it, and it hit the ground and rolled up toward third base.

Rory, who had taken a lead off second, steamed into third. The pitcher retrieved the ball and threw to first. He threw too high. The first baseman couldn't get the ball, which went to the dugout, and Rory came in to tie the score. Coach Mack, with a man on second as a result of the overthrow into the dugout, now put in a pinch hitter for Spider. The pinch hitter walked, and Ken Ishiwara came up to hit a grounder between the third baseman and the shortstop, which went all the way out to near center field, to score Harter. White's Beach was now one run ahead, the score being 4-3. But that was the end of the big inning, for Stammers, the next batter, flied out.

Now Ron Fields had to be sent in to pitch. He took his warm-up pitches and looked real good. The first batter he struck out and the second he walked. The third was hit by the first pitch, putting two men on base with one out. Then the El Redondo bench jockeys got on the pitcher shouting, "Hey, Ron. You're gone," at the top of their voices. This was the signal for White's Beach to retaliate trying to upset the hitter, a thin tall youngster, but with a lot of power.

"Swing, swing, dingaling," they shouted.

The batter swung, and the ball seethed past Ron, over the shortstop's head to drop in midfield and score the man on second, tying the score, 4-4, still with only one out and now a man on second and a man on first. The next batter walked, and Al Harter went out for a conference with the pitcher in which Coach Sevri joined.

"What's the trouble?" asked Sevri.

"Lost my rhythm," said Ron.

"Knee troubling you?"

"When I try a fast ball, I get a pain in my shoulder. Kind of a pull."

"You're releasing early," said Joe. "Your follow-through is off. Keep your back straight. I think you're trying to favor your knee, and it's affecting your delivery. You've got bases loaded and only one out. What do you think?"

"I think I can hold them," said Ron.

The conference broke up and Ron struck out the next batter with a change-up, a slider, and a medium fast ball on the inside corner. But then his control went entirely and he walked the next batter, bringing in a run.

174

Coach Mack looked gloomily around the dugout and signaled Coco, who had been doing a little pitching practice in the bullpen. "How do you feel?" he asked.

"Terrible," said Coco.

"Me too," said Coach Mack. "Two outs. Bases loaded. It's your problem. All I ask of you is don't walk anybody."

Coco walked out to the mound wondering why he had ever decided he wanted to be a pitcher. Halfway there he turned and headed back to the dugout.

"It's okay," said Coach Mack, anticipating his request. "Rory will catch you."

Chapter Eighteen

It was at this point in the game that Mr. Hurley arrived back from Los Angeles. He made his way into the stands, and his son Kevin filled him in on the situation.

"It's do or die for Coco again," said Kevin. "But this time, though the bases are loaded, there are two outs. They're one run ahead and this is the bottom of the fifth. White's Beach gets one more turn at bat."

"Same old deal," said a man behind them. "We can never beat El Redondo. And now they've put in that stupid kid who walks everybody."

Mr. Hurley turned around and saw Mr. Melotti behind him. "That stupid kid is my son," he said.

"Sure wish he'd open his eyes when he throws the ball," said Mr. Melotti.

This time Coco's warm-up pitches were almost respectable. Only two were wild, bringing jeers from the El Redondo dugout. Rory didn't have to go over the signals with his brother. He squatted down behind the plate and said to the batter, "Whatever you do, don't pop up. This will be a fast ball." It was. The batter swung and foul tipped it over the backstop.

"See," said Rory. "I wouldn't give you a bum steer. Now this will be a change-up." The batter didn't believe him. It was a change-up and the batter swung ahead of the pitch for strike two.

"Always the straight stuff from me," said Rory. "That's what they call me. Honest John. But my name's Rory really. That kid's my brother and . . ." The batter called for time and stepped out of the box. When he stepped in again and got set Rory started the patter all over again. "Get set for another fast ball," he said, "because that's what I'm calling for."

But this time it was a change-up and the batter wasn't fooled. He was expecting the change-up and swung. Mr. Hurley shut his eyes. Mr. Melotti behind him said, "That stupid kid . . ." The ball soared away to center field and, just as it was about to clear the fence, Al Harter leaped and caught it, bringing everyone in the White's Beach stands to their feet, cheering.

It was a great catch. As soon as the ball was hit, Al had started streaking for the fence with his back to the ball, and turned around to leap and catch it at the last moment. It was easily the greatest play of the All-Star games to date and gave White's Beach a chance to stay alive. The score was 5–4 El Redondo, but White's Beach now had its last turn at bat.

Melotti was to lead off, and on the first pitch he hit a shot to the third baseman, who couldn't quite get to the ball, and Tony got on base. Then came Green, who struck out. The next batter was Martin, who was a good hitter, with as good an eye as Ken Ishiwara. If there was one thing he didn't want to do, it was hit into a double play, and to avoid this, he moved his right foot just a little nearer to the plate to pivot his shoulders around when he swung.

But he was expecting a change-up, swung late, and the ball soared way out to right field. The right fielder came over and made the catch, and Melotti, who was not a fast runner, held on first. Two outs and nothing to show for it but a man on first base. The El Redondo dugout started yelling as Randy Day came up.

"What's it like to be the last out?" they shouted, and "Down the drain—again."

Randy glanced at the coach, got the sign to swing and swung on the first pitch. He connected solidly. The ball cleared the first baseman and dropped before the charging right fielder could get to it, and Randy was aboard and White's Beach still alive—but only just.

Now it was the catcher's spot, and Rory stepped into the box, his mouth as dry as chalk.

"Swing zwing, dingaling," yelled El Redondo, and, "Rory, Rory. No glory."

Rory's favorite pitch was letter high and outside, and he decided to wait for it. He took on the first two pitches, which were strikes, and the catcalls from El Redondo rose to a crescendo. Then came two balls, and at that point Rory called for time and, rubbing a handful of dirt on the bat, stole a look around the outfield. They were playing him straight away, but there was a bit of a hole between the right and center fielders. He stepped back into the box and the catcher said, "This is it feller. You're dead." The pitcher went into his windup and threw and it was just what Rory had hoped for—about letter high and on the outside corner. He connected and there was no doubt about where the ball was going. It was a home run over the right-field fence—a home run with two on, putting White's Beach two runs ahead and no more at bats unless the game was tied.

"Okay, Coco," said Coach Mack when the furor in the dugout had died down. "See if you can get yourself a little more insurance." But Coco popped out on the first pitch and went out to the mound to try to protect the win—the first win, if it came off, that White's Beach had ever scored over El Redondo.

He started off badly. He tried to throw fast strikes, and the result was that he walked the first runner, and the second man got on a "Texas Leaguer" that just cleared the shortstop's head. Rory went out to confer with him.

"Forget the fast ball," he said. "You don't have it. Just get it somewhere near the strike zone. These guys are just as uptight as you."

"If they were as uptight as me," said Coco, "they'd look like walnuts."

"Just do your best," said Rory. "Keep it low."

Coco got two strikes on the next batter and then two balls in a row. He tried a fast ball and it was fouled off. He tried a change-up and it was fouled off. He tried a curve and that was fouled off too. Then he threw the Krazy Kevin pitch, or tried to, but it turned into a wild pitch and the runner on second advanced to third and there were still no outs.

"Here goes," thought Coco and tried with a change-up. The hitter was not expecting it, but he swung. The ball zoomed back to Coco who caught it and threw immediately to third. It wasn't the world's best throw, but the third baseman grabbed the ball and stepped on the bag to make the out. The White's

Beach dugout exploded with cheering and there was pandemonium in the stands. Two outs and one to go.

"Don't those kids ever get into just an ordinary ball game?" demanded Mr. Hurley of Kevin.

"I wish that stupid kid could throw strikes," said Mr. Melotti.

"That stupid kid's my son," said Mr. Hurley.

"I know," said Mr. Melotti. "I sure wish he could throw strikes."

Coco, back on the mound, took two or three good breaths and went into a windup. The first pitch was wild and went to the backstop. The runner on second got to third. Rory didn't even bother to walk the ball back to Coco. There wasn't anything he could say to him that would improve the situation. The count went to three balls, no strikes and then Coco got two strikes on the batter.

"One more strike," yelled the stands and the dugout. "Just one more strike."

Rory called for a fast ball and Coco shook him off He shook off a change-up and a curve and a fast ball again, and when at last Rory called for the Krazy Kevin pitch Coco nodded his head. Rory called for time and walked out to him.

"Look," he said. "If you throw that crazy pitch and it doesn't work, that runner on third is coming home. Why don't you throw him something he can hit—

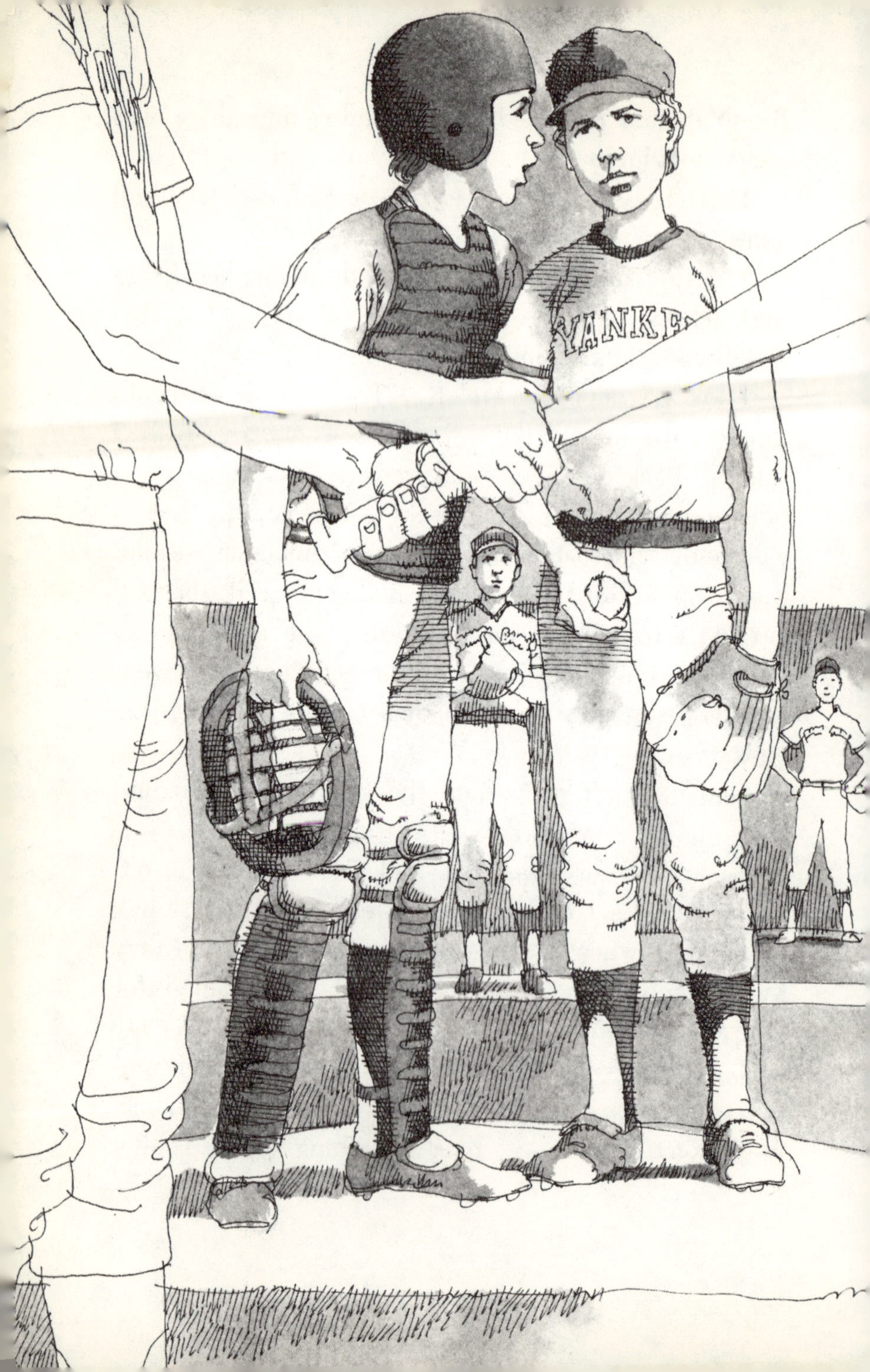

bring it up a little so it'll be a fly ball and an easy out."

"You got money for a hot dog? My stomach feels awful empty," said Coco.

"Hot dog?" said Rory. "What's a hot dog got to do with it? Just give me a fast ball. Anything but that crazy pitch."

"Okay," said Coco. "But if they hit it over the fence, I'm going to tell you about it every day for a month."

Rory went back to the plate. "Fast ball," he said to the batter. "He wants to throw that crazy pitch of his and I told him fast ball."

Coco went into his windup with a fast ball in mind, but right then he remembered what Kevin had said to him so often early in the year. "Back off. Don't try so hard." So he held up on the fast ball, and what resulted was a perfect Krazy Kevin pitch. The batter went into a swing and held up, and the ball danced under his bat and across the plate.

"Strike three," cried the umpire. "You're out," and the whole White's Beach dugout exploded across the field to grab Coco and carry him in shoulder high.

Mr. Hurley turned around to Mr. Melotti. Mr. Melotti looked him right in the eye and said, "You know something? That stupid kid of yours is one heck of a pitcher."

Chapter Nineteen

White's Beach won three more games which put them in the semifinals for the state championship. But then their luck—and everybody admitted that they'd had their share of it—ran out and a central California team from Mill Valley scored a home run with two men on in the bottom of the fifth to put them three runs ahead. When White's Beach came to bat at the top of the sixth, they drew a blank, and that was it. They were out of the race.

But nobody was depressed. The team had done what no White's Beach team had ever done before—beaten El Redondo and got into the state semifinals. It was a tremendous achievement which received plenty of public acknowledgment in the city. A Recreation Department banquet was held in their honor at which they received a special trophy from the city and plaques for each of the team members. Rory and Coco brought their plaques home and put them up on the shelf next to the surfing and basketball trophies they'd received.

The day after the banquet and presentation Mr. Hurley inquired where his two sons were.

"Surfing," said his wife.

Mr. Hurley sighed. "Let's see," he said, "it goes baseball, surfing, football, basketball, and then baseball again."

"More or less," said his wife. "But you left out volleyball and kite flying—and somewhere in there there's yo-yos."

Later came a letter from Mr. Truxton of Western Pipe regretting that the vacancy for which Mr. Hurley had applied had been filled, but assuring him that his application would be kept on file. Two further interviews were also fruitless, and Mr. Hurley felt more and more depressed about his prospects and began to wonder whether he hadn't been wrong in putting his family ahead of his job and leaving his old employer —though when he thought more deeply about the matter, he always concluded that he was right. Then one day he received an unexpected long-distance telephone call.

"Mr. Hurley," said the caller. "We had a date for

lunch in Honolulu some months ago. What happened?"

"Mr. Li," cried Mr. Hurley. "How good to hear from you. How is everything going with you?"

"Fine. But you haven't been back here in a long time. Why is that?"

"Well," said Mr. Hurley. "It's a long story. But business has not been going well. To be frank, my company hoped to get a big order from the Kona Coffee Growers, and I missed on that. So it was decided to move me to Arizona, and since my home is in White's Beach—well, I'm no longer with them."

"That is what I heard," said Mr. Li. "And I am sorry to hear it. But also I am glad. The Orchid Growers Association, with some of whose members you had lunch and played golf now and again, decided recently to expand their sales representation on the West Coast and asked me to recommend a man to put in charge. Naturally, I thought of you. But I did not know whether I could get you away from your old company. You told me they were a fine company and you were satisfied with them."

"They are a good company," said Mr. Hurley. "I worked for them fourteen years. They are one of the best. I just didn't want to move to Arizona."

"How about moving to Hawaii?" asked Mr. Li.

"Twenty thousand dollars a year, plus expenses and a good commission on sales."

"Mr. Li, do I have to move to Hawaii?" asked Mr. Hurley.

"Mr. Hurley, don't you like Hawaii?" asked Mr. Li.

"Yes I do," said Mr. Hurley. "But White's Beach is our home. All our kids were born here. All their friends live here. My kids just wouldn't like to give up this place."

There was a slight pause and Mr. Li said, "That is what I wanted to hear. In the flower business, people come first. Flowers don't buy flowers. People buy flowers, and my associates and I agreed that we had to have someone who had truly human values in charge of our organization on the West Coast; someone who can think of the happiness and pleasure of others, which is the reason for giving flowers in the first instance. So Mr. Hurley, you have passed our most important test, and you have the job if you want it. But do you know what recommended you for the job in the first instance, Mr. Hurley?"

"My golf?"

"No, you play worse golf than I do. The Little League Pancake Breakfast. Yes. The Pancake Breakfast. So much concern for young people that you could fly from Hawaii back to Los Angeles just to help with a pancake breakfast. That was your best recommendation for the job. As I said, flowers are for people, and those who sell flowers have to care about people. When can you come to Honolulu to settle the matter?"

"Mr. Li," said Mr. Hurley. "I'll be there tomorrow."

Mr. Hurley put down the telephone and went into the kitchen where his wife was working.

"Remember the first orchid I gave you?" he asked.

"Yes. At the high school Senior Prom. How could I forget it. It was the first orchid I ever had in my life."

"Well, now you can have all the orchids you want," said Mr. Hurley, and told her about the job.

"I'm not surprised at all," said his wife quietly. "I'm not the teeniest bit surprised. It's exactly what you deserve." And then she burst into tears.

Much later that year, at the end of the basketball season, Rory and Coco approached their father diffidently after dinner.

"Dad," they said, "maybe you won't want to do this, but we've all been asked to try to get our parents to come to an important meeting tonight."

Mr. Hurley looked up from a report he was working on. The words sounded slightly familiar.

"What kind of a meeting?" he asked.

"Baseball," said Rory. "It's to elect a board . . ."

"I know," said Mr. Hurley. He looked sternly at his two sons. "Did you wash the dog?" he asked.

Rory looked at Coco and Coco said, "Yes . . . that is . . . last week."

Mr. Hurley sighed. "Okay," he said. "Okay. And I'll tell you something. I'm probably going to be the only guy in the history of Little League baseball in this city who will actually volunteer to run the Pancake Breakfast."

LEONARD WIBBERLEY is an extremely successful novelist who has written a large number of juvenile and adult books. He is most well-remembered for his book *The Mouse that Roared,* which was made into a movie.